It Was Becoming Dangerous...
Playing House With Julian.

It was too fun and too easy. "Is your brother looking this way, Jules?"

"I don't know. I'm looking at you."

It was the tone he used, deep and husky as a country love song, that made her almost forget that this was just an act.

"I'm pretty sure he's watching," she whispered, moving closer to Julian's ear. She leaned against his chest and whispered, "I'm thinking we could just stroll off somewhere private and return a little disheveled, you know. Let his imagination run wild with jealousy."

She could feel the coiled tension in the muscles underneath Julian's shirt as he dropped his head to whisper back into her ear, his lips grazing the lobe. "As you wish."

Dear Reader,

I'm sure you've noticed our exciting new look! Harlequin Desire novels will now feature a brand-new cover design, one that perfectly captures the dramatic and sensual stories you love.

Nothing else about the Harlequin Desire books has changed. Inside our pages, you'll still find wealthy alpha heroes caught in unforgettable stories of scandal, secrets and seduction.

Don't miss any of this month's sizzling reads....

CANYON by Brenda Jackson
(The Westmorelands)

DEEP IN A TEXAN'S HEART by Sara Orwig
(Texas Cattleman's Club)

THE BABY DEAL by Kat Cantrell
(Billionaires & Babies)

WRONG MAN, RIGHT KISS by Red Garnier

HIS INSTANT HEIR by Katherine Garbera
(Baby Business)

HIS BY DESIGN by Dani Wade

I hope you're as pleased with our new look as we are. Drop by www.Harlequin.com or use the hash tag #harlequindesire on Twitter to let us know what you think.

Stacy Boyd

Senior Editor

Harlequin Desire

RED GARNIER

———

WRONG MAN, RIGHT KISS

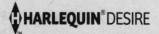

As always, with my deepest thanks to everyone
at Harlequin Desire—who make the best team of editors
I've ever come across! Thank you for making this book shine.

This book is dedicated to my flesh-and-blood hero and
our two little ones, who, it turns out, are not so little anymore.

ISBN-13: 978-0-373-73261-6

Recycling programs
for this product may
not exist in your area.

WRONG MAN, RIGHT KISS

HARLEQUIN®
™ www.Harlequin.com

Printed in U.S.A.

Books by Red Garnier

Harlequin Desire

Wrong Man, Right Kiss #2248

Silhouette Desire

The Secretary's Bossman Bargain #2028
Paper Marriage Proposition #2064

RED GARNIER

is a fan of books, chocolate and happily-ever-afters. What better way to spend the day than combining all three? Traveling frequently between the United States and Mexico, Red likes to call Texas home. She'd love to hear from her readers at redgarnier@gmail.com. For more on upcoming books and current contests, please visit her website, www.redgarnier.com.

Dear Reader,

I've always had a thing about connections. Best friends share such special connections that are among the strongest I've ever known. As strong as blood ties and sometimes even stronger, for you choose your friends rather than "inherit" them. Friends are with you through good and bad, through heartbreak and tears, through anger and despair, through laughter and fun. Friends know secrets that even lovers sometimes don't. They see and know you at your best and at your worst. Therefore, I think some of the most amazing love stories in the world are among best friends.

Julian and Molly have been best friends their entire lives. They know everything about each other, things that even their family members don't know. Seeing how they genuinely care for each other and always protect each other (while oblivious to the extent of their true feelings) has to make this book among the most fun, most heartwarming stories I've ever written. I seriously hope you enjoy it as much as I did!

With love,

Red

One

Molly Devaney needed a hero.

She could think of no other way to solve her dilemma.

She'd been tossing and turning at night for the past two weeks, obsessing over what she'd done, wishing and praying and hoping she could figure out how to fix things and fix them fast.

It had taken fifteen days and fifteen hellish nights to come to the conclusion that she needed some help—and pronto—and there was only one man who could save the day, just like he'd previously saved her on plenty of other days.

Her hero of all times, ever since she was three and he was six, and Molly and her sister, Kate, recently orphaned, had ended up living with his rich and wonderful family in their San Antonio mansion.

Julian John Gage.

Okay. The guy was definitely no saint. He was a ladies' man down to his very sexy bones. He could have any woman he wanted, in any way he preferred, at any time he felt like, and the stupid meathead *knew* this. Which meant he was determined to sample them *all*.

It really rankled her sometimes.

But while he was an incorrigible rake with the ladies, a handful to the press due to his position as head of PR for the *San Antonio Daily,* a problem to his brothers and a bane to his own mother, to Molly, Julian John Gage was nothing short of the bomb. He was her greatest friend, the reason she'd never really found a man until now and the only person on this earth who would be honest enough to tell her how to seduce his hardheaded, annoying older brother.

The problem now was that Molly could've found a better time to expose her wicked plans to him. Bursting into his apartment on a Sunday morning was not her brightest idea. But then she was losing precious time and urgently needed Garrett, his older brother, to realize he loved her before she all but died from the misery of it all.

Now, if only Julian would stop staring at her as if she'd lost it big-time—which he'd been doing for the past couple of minutes, ever since she'd blurted out her plans.

The guy just stood there, easily the most magnificent work of art in his flawless contemporary apartment, his feet braced apart and his steely jaw hanging slightly ajar.

"I can't have heard right." When at last he spoke, his husky morning voice was laden with incredulousness. "Did you just ask me to help you seduce my own brother?"

Molly stopped pacing around the coffee table and, all of a sudden, she felt very much like a tramp. "Well…I didn't actually say *seduce.* Did I?"

An awkward silence followed as they both thought back to five minutes ago. Julian lifted a lone eyebrow. "You didn't?"

Molly sighed. She couldn't remember, either. She'd been a little tongue-tied when the living sculpture—aka Julian—had opened the door, gloriously bare-chested and wearing only a pair of low-slung drawstring linen pajama pants. The pants were so low-slung and sheer, in fact, that Molly could clearly make out the dark V of hair starting just under Julian's flat, bronzed navel, a tidbit which was playing havoc with her mind since she'd never seen a man partly naked before.

Plus, Julian was not just any man. He looked more like David Beckham's younger brother.

The hotter one.

Good thing their friendship made Molly immune.

"Okay, maybe I did say that, I can't remember." Molly shook her head and fought to get back on track. "It's only that I've just realized I need to do something drastic before some bimbo steals him from me for good. I need to get him, Julian. And you're the expert seducer, so I need *you* to tell me what to do."

His eyes—green like the leaves of the oaks outside— flared slightly in concern. "Look, Molls. I don't quite know how to explain this to you, so let me just get it out there." He started pacing. "We all grew up together. My brothers and I saw you in diapers. There's no way Garrett will ever look at you and see anything else but a little sister, the key words here being *little* and *sister.*"

"All right, so it's too late to do anything about the Pampers issue, I get it, but I have solid reasons to believe Garrett's feelings toward me have changed! I mean, has he ever even said he only thinks of me as a little sister, Julian? I'm already twenty-three. He may actually think I've grown up to be quite a sophisticated and sexy lady." *With really nice breasts that he quite happily fondled at the masquerade,* she thought smugly.

But Julian regarded her attire—certainly not one of her best outfits, she'd grant him that—with a look that was the opposite of thrilled.

"Your sister, Kate, is sophisticated and sexy. But you?" He stared pointedly at her boho skirt and paint-splattered tank top, then plunged his hand through his sun-streaked hair as though supremely frustrated. "God, Molls, have you stopped by a mirror recently? You look like you've been smacked, kicked, then put for a spin inside a blender."

"Julian John Gage!" Molly gasped, so genuinely hurt her heart constricted. "My next New York solo exhibit happens to be in four weeks—I don't have time to care about how I look! Plus I can't believe you're giving me crap about my work clothes when you stand there half nak—"

A door slammed shut in the depths of the apartment, and Molly whirled around with a scowl, ready to keep shouting. But she spotted someone approaching out of the corner of her eye and in that instant, she lost all power of speech. That someone was, of course, a woman.

The leggiest, blondest blonde Molly had ever seen was currently stepping out of Julian's bedroom. She was carrying a gold clutch purse and wearing a pair of crimson stilettos and one of Julian's button-down shirts, which seemed to barely contain what was easily a set of enormous breasts that made Molly's girls suddenly shrink before her eyes.

Now *that* woman looked as if she'd been inside a blender. But at a really marvelous speed. Molly wished she could pull off that tumbled look so well.

"I have to go," the mystery woman told Julian sultrily from afar. "I left my number on your pillow, so…" She made the universal call-me sign and puckered her lips. "It was really nice meeting you last night. I hope you don't mind me borrowing a shirt? My dress didn't seem to fare as well as I did." She released a soft giggle, and when Julian remained unmoved by her sexiness and Molly only gaped, she gracefully crossed the room to leave.

The instant the elevator doors shut behind her, Molly's gaze jerked back to Julian. "Seriously?" Annoyance flared through her with such force that she stalked forward and shoved his rigid shoulder. That *womanizer!* "Seriously, Julian? Do you have to sleep with every woman you meet?"

She shoved him again, but his shoulder budged as much as a concrete building would.

With a rumbling chuckle, Julian grabbed her hand and forced her fingers into a fist. "We aren't talking about my love life. We're talking about yours." He frowned down at their fisted hands and briskly released her. "And the fact that you have paint on your nose, in your hair and on your shoes, and this starving-artist look is not going to do anything for my brother."

Molly shot him a harsh glare, then shoved past him and stormed down the hall. "Oh, just let me grab one of your shirts! I'm sure that will do wonders for my pitifully *un*sexy and *un*sophisticated looks."

"Aw, heck. Molly! Come on, Molls. Moo, baby. Get back here and just let me wrap my head around all this, all right? You know you've always been pretty, and I know that's why you don't give a damn."

Julian reached her in three long strides, promptly snatched her arm and dragged her back to the living room. Molly glared at him at first, but when she heard the low, deep sigh that worked its way up his chest, the sigh that said he just didn't know what to do with her anymore, her anger vanished.

It was just too hard to stay angry with Julian John.

Molly knew he'd do anything for her—and maybe that was why she was here. On a Sunday morning. And why she continued to be a pain in his great-looking butt. Because nobody had ever done the things that Julian John had done to make sure she was safe and protected, except maybe her sister, who had practically assumed the role of a mother when they were orphaned.

Kate had put her through school, coddled her, raised her and loved her every second of growing up without a mom and a dad. So the fact that Julian had been there for her almost as much as Kate said a lot about a man who insisted on pretending he was nothing but a playboy.

Which he first and foremost was.

But that was precisely why Molly was happy that he was just her friend and *not* the man she had set her romantic sights on.

"Look," she said as he released her, feeling herself blush as she remembered her and Garrett's stolen kiss. "I know you might not understand this. But I love your brother so much, I—"

"Since freaking when, Molls? He's always annoyed the crap out of both of us."

She stiffened defensively. "True, okay. But that was when he was so rigid, you know. Before."

"Before what?"

"Before…before I realized that he…" *Wants me. Before he said the things he said to me when he kissed me.* Her stomach wrenched at the painful memory. Anxiously, she pushed her red tresses back behind her shoulders and tried again. "I—I really can't explain it, but something has monumentally changed. And I just know he loves me back, I just know it in my soul, Julian—please don't laugh."

She couldn't bring herself to look him in the eyes for some inexplicable reason, so she spun around and slumped down on the leather sofa. The silence ticked by, and within seconds, she became aware of some extremely strange vibes coming from the vicinity of where Julian stood.

The laugh that broke the silence was worst of all. It was anything but mirthful. "I can't freaking believe this."

Molly held her breath and peered up at him, finding that a harsh frown had settled on his strong, tanned face. She had never seen Julian truly mad, but if that black scowl was a good indicator, he was getting there, and fast.

Her stomach clenched when she once again took a peek at his flat, muscled navel, the dark V dipping into those superloose drawstring pants and leading into— Okay, enough of that. She had to focus on getting Garrett. *Now.*

"Julian…" She really had to say something. Sighing, she signaled at that perfectly tanned, perfectly perfect torso. "Look. While we discuss this, can you put on one of your remaining shirts? The chest and the six-pack and all that you've got going on are just… Let's just say it makes me want to go take a peek at Garrett."

Julian scoffed and flexed seriously impressive biceps. "You know damned well my brother doesn't have these guns."

"He does, too."

He flexed his other biceps. "I may be his baby brother, but I can take the guy down in five seconds flat with these."

"Oh, puleeze. The only thing you're probably better at doing than him is screwing around—and you *deserve* that after saying I look like I live in a blender."

"Ahh. So once again, you missed the part where I said you were pretty." Julian fell down on a chair and for a long moment, they sat there, both staring pensively into space.

When he at last spoke, Molly was relieved to hear that his voice had regained its usual playful note. "Yeah. You're right. I am better at screwing around than both my brothers put together. Not that Landon would ever look at another woman now that he's married."

He leaned back and watched her with the beginnings of a smile that carried a hint of danger while he linked his hands behind his head in a deceptively relaxed pose.

"So let's screw around with Garrett. Why not? He's always been ridiculously protective of you and Kate. He'd go Donkey Kong if he ever found out you were dating someone. Especially someone with a bad reputation. You don't even really have to date the guy, just make him agree to play your doting lover for a while, ask him to be convincing enough to yank ole Garrett's chain."

Delighted that Julian was at last addressing her predicament, Molly almost jumped out of her seat and found herself clapping twice. "Yes! Yes! He sounds charming. But the question is, do I actually know such a man?"

Julian's smile was perfectly wolfish. "Baby, you're looking right at him."

His words appeared to strike Molly like an electric shock, and Julian wondered if that was a good thing, a bad thing or totally irrelevant to his newly hatched plan.

"Excuse me?" She jerked upright on his couch and gripped the leather cushions with such force that it looked as if she was on a roller-coaster ride. "I'm sure I heard wrong. Did you just offer to be my boyfriend or something?"

"Or something," Julian agreed, his lips curling upward.

He knew he looked calm. Collected. But inside his head, the wheels were turning with particularly inspiring ideas. Ideas he might later regret. But they were still damned good.

"Wh-what do you mean 'or something'?" she asked him.

Julian could hardly get over how adorable she looked

sitting there, shocked and disbelieving as if she'd just won the Megabucks.

Her eyes were just so wide and so damned blue you'd have to be made of freaking stone not to be willing to move mountains for her. Honestly, he'd never seen such expressive, genuinely innocent eyes in his life. It was a guarantee that Molly would lose every poker game she ever played, her expressions were so real and so clear. Hell, just the way she *looked* at him with those eyes made him feel like some sort of superhero. Not even his own mother gazed at him like Molly did.

With an amused smile, one he sometimes found himself wearing when he was with her, he explained, "'Or something' means I don't have girlfriends, Molly. I have lovers. And I'd be happy to pretend to be yours."

He'd meant to emphasize the word *pretend,* but somehow when he spoke, the only word he seemed to be able to emphasize was *yours.*

Because obviously he would only ever do this kind of stuff for Molly.

"You're kidding me, Jules," she said as she somberly scanned his face. She was not even moving, had practically become a statue on the couch.

He might have laughed at that, except to his own disbelief and amazement, he was dead serious. Dead. As *heck.* Serious. And now he needed to know if *she* was, too. "I may like to kid around, Molls, but I wouldn't kid you with this."

"So you're prepared to pretend to be in love with me?"

He nodded, and his hands itched to wipe away a green smudge of paint from her forehead and a red one from her cheek. "I figure I've probably done worse, Moo. Like that girl who just left…not really prime in the head, if you get me."

He tapped his forehead, but she wasn't even paying attention.

As though in a trance, Molly rose to her feet, all five feet of chaotic red hair and heavy turquoise necklaces and creamy paint-streaked skin, her eyes shining as his proposal finally seemed to dawn on her. "And Garrett will see us together and be madly jealous! Oh, my God, yes, yes, this is brilliant, Julian! How long do you think it will take to get him to realize he loves me? A couple of days? A week?"

Julian stared at her in silence. She really sounded... enamored. Didn't she?

He thought about it for a bit, and with each passing second, he grew more and more baffled. Suddenly all he wanted was for somebody to please tell him what in the *hell* was going on here. Was this some sort of lame-ass *joke?* Molly? Dreaming about his older brother? For real?

If the ten-year age difference wasn't an issue, the fact that the Gages had grown up with strict codes of conduct regarding the Devaney girls should matter. And tons. Especially to Garrett, who never, ever broke a rule. Had his brother done something to give Molly the impression of being interested?

Dammit, this just struck him as so, so wrong, he didn't even know where to begin.

His brother Garrett was ridiculously overprotective of the Devaney girls. The reason they'd become orphans in the first place was because their only living parent, who had been the Gages' bodyguard, had died in the line of duty protecting Julian's father and Garrett from an armed gang hired by the Mexican mafia to murder Julian's father for newspaper coverage disclosing their names and operations. But the Gages' bodyguard had died protecting Garrett, too. Though the gang members had been sentenced to life in prison, as the lone survivor of that bloody night two decades ago, Garrett had been sentenced to a life in hell.

Now he lived with a boatload of guilt and regret. When their widowed mother had taken the girls under their wing, Garrett had been rabid to protect them, even, apparently, from Julian—who had liked to tickle the hell out of Molly and make her giggle… Well, Garrett had always ridden Julian's goddamn back about the rules where the Devaney sisters were concerned. This annoyed not only Julian but also Molly—who loved being tickled by him.

So now, after Molly had complained a thousand times that Garrett never let Julian and her have any fun, it was damned hard to believe that she suddenly had the hots for Garrett.

What in the hell was that about?

Julian and Molly were friends. Honest-to-God, die-for-you, chase-a-killer-for-you and do-all-kinds-of-strange-stuff-for-you friends.

Julian was Molly's one, two and three on her freaking speed dial. The first number was for his office, the second for his cell phone and the third for his home. Molly even frequently admitted that their friendship was better than a romantic relationship, and it sure as hell had lasted longer than any marriage these days.

But after hearing her profess her love for Garrett several times today, Julian had realized that if she was serious— and apparently she was—he would have to help her.

He was going to "help" her realize that she was not in love with Garrett Gage. *Period.*

"I think we can get Garrett where we want him in about a month," he finally assured her, gazing deeply into her eyes in an attempt to gauge how deeply in love she believed herself to be. Knowing what a romantic Molly was, he actually dreaded the answer.

Hell, she was probably already hearing wedding bells; she looked positively love-struck. Which just hit the wrong chord with him. Oh, boy, did it ever.

"Do you really think he'll go for it? He's so difficult to read most of the time," Molly said in a dubious tone.

"Molly, no man in his right mind would stand by and watch his brother put his paws on his girl."

Blushing in excitement, Molly leaped forward and hugged him tight, kissing his stubbled cheek. "You'd really do this just for me? You're the best, Jules. Thank you so much."

As her slim, warm arms tightened around his narrow waist, Julian's entire frame stiffened as if she'd just zapped him. He was naked from the waist up, and he suddenly could feel Molly everywhere he didn't want to. Warm and smelling of sweet things.

Worst of all was that she snuggled in comfortably, turned her face into his neck and whispered, "You're the best part of my life, you know that, Jules? I never know how to thank you properly for everything you do."

Was she for real?

Because the ideas those words put into his head were so, so wrong, Julian could've shot himself.

He tried remembering his past lovers' names, in alphabetical order, but still could not relax a single inch until Molly extracted herself.

Letting go a long, long breath, he avoided her inquisitive gaze and grumbled, "Don't thank me yet, Molls. Let's just see how it goes, all right?"

"It'll go splendidly, Julian, I just know it. Before the month ends, I'll probably be wearing an engagement ring."

He rolled his eyes because he still could not even believe this was happening. "Well, let's not call the wedding planner yet, all right? Just remember that for this month, you're with me, and heads up, baby, the rest of my family isn't going to be too happy about it."

She frowned in puzzlement and planted her hands on her hips. "Why on earth not? Am I not good enough for you?"

"No, Molls. It's me." He turned to gaze sightlessly out the window as a heaviness settled painfully atop his chest. "They think I'm no good for you."

Two

"You're jerking me around, toad, I just know it!"

Julian leaned back in his swivel chair and suppressed a smile as he watched his brother pace across the state-of-the-art conference room on the top floor of the *San Antonio Daily,* a thriving business the Gage family had run since the 1930s.

"Brother," Julian tsked, "I realize I'm younger than you, but don't forget I *am* stronger and I *will* take you down if you keep pissing me off."

"So you're basically admitting that you're sleeping with our little Molls?"

"I never said that. I said we're dating and she's moving in with me." This last was something Julian hadn't discussed with Molly before, but it had suddenly seemed like a good idea. And when Garrett's complexion turned the color of a ripe cherry tomato, Julian knew he'd struck the jackpot.

Garrett was livid.

Julian and Molly had discussed some basic rules yesterday—like no dating anyone else, a good dose of PDA for show when around family and strangers, and how neither would ever, ever disclose to anyone that their romantic liaison had been fake. This seemed especially important to Molly, who seemed to think it of utmost importance to be convincing in their new "relationship."

Julian was right on board with that.

Hell, he was on board with anything that meant pushing Garrett's buttons.

Not that he had anything against the guy, except the fact that he was maybe too honorable for his own damned good, and ever since Landon, the eldest brother, had embarked on a much deserved sixty-day honeymoon, Garrett seemed to think he carried the weight of the world on his shoulders. Or at least, of the family business.

There was plenty of love among the three, yeah, but Julian had been planning to exact a special brotherly revenge on Garrett for a long. Long. Time.

A revenge made all the sweeter by the fact that Molly suddenly had it in her pretty head to get Garrett's *personal attention*.

Hell, Julian hadn't had a wink of sleep last night just thinking about it.

Now he took a moment to enjoy the fact that his brother's face was taut with displeasure, his knuckles jutting out as he gripped his coffee cup. He stopped his pacing and stood across from Julian at the conference table, where they'd just wrapped up a meeting with their top executives. "Since when are you two interested in each other?" Garrett demanded.

"Since we started sexting," Julian returned, unflinching. Then, before Garrett could ask more, Julian lifted his cell phone and read a message. "Damn, this girl turns me on." He pretended to text Molly back and took his sweet, sweet time about it. Though in reality he was just telling her:

He knows. Guy's going bananas. Tell you about it @ dinner.

Garrett shot him a murderous glare. "Does Kate know about this sexting/moving-in...relationship?"

"Probably, unless she's too busy catering for her next event. She is Molly's sister, after all."

Just then, Molly's response popped up:

No wonder Kate and Garrett get along so well.

Julian quickly typed in:

I suppose Kate no longer worships the ground I tread on?

Molly replied:

Affirmative. Be careful, lover. She has a spatula and she's not afraid to use it as a weapon.

Julian's lips curled in amusement. Ahh, Molly. Light of his life.

"So which part was it?"

Julian gazed blankly up at Garrett, who almost had steam coming out of his ears. "Which part was what?" he asked.

"Which part of what Mother, Landon and I have been telling you for, oh...say, two decades, did you not *get?* The part that Molly Devaney was *hands-off?* The part that you could be *disowned* if you harmed her in any way?"

Julian nodded to placate him. "I heard you all. I heard you the first time, the tenth time, the hundredth time and I hear you now. Now hear this, bro." He leaned forward across the conference table and scowled. "I don't. Freaking. Care. Do *you*...get *that?*"

Garrett clenched his jaw and drew in a breath that inflated his chest. The guy was so rankled, he was probably about a step away from banging his chest like Tarzan. "I'm going to have words with Molly, as I am sure it is in her best interests to reconsider this stupidity. Just know this, Julian...if you hurt her, if you so much as harm a hair on her head..."

He didn't know if it was the threat, or the possessive way Garrett was acting toward Molly or the simple fact that Molly fancied herself in love with the guy. Worse, he feared it might be due to the fact that Garrett wanted Molly for himself. But Julian's cool began to fade, and it took an inhuman effort to keep the mask on his face.

Suddenly transported back to his teenage years, he too easily remembered all those damned times he and Molly tried to get close. The special bond you forged with someone, one that is rare and precious and you'd be lucky to find in your lifetime—Julian had always had that with her. But every time their friendship threatened to develop into something more romantic, his family would panic and they'd swoop down like vultures to emotionally blackmail, harass and coerce him to keep them apart. More than once, he'd even been sent abroad for months, the first time apparently because Julian had been "looking" at Molly in a way that neither Kate, Landon, nor their mother—and especially not Garrett—had liked.

Julian had told himself time and again that he didn't care. And once he was an adult, they'd made him believe he was a playboy until he had no other choice but to play the part. He could have any woman—they always told him—except Kate or Molly. That was the rule.

And every year of his life, that single, simple rule had made him feel tied up, caged like a lion, and as unhappy as a penned-up bull.

Now the command from his brother to stay away from the only woman who truly knew him made a fresh surge of anger rise up from within him. No matter what Molly thought now, or what Garrett planned to do, this was Julian's future on the line—and he had been planning it for years. No one was going to mess with that future. Or with his red-haired, paint-streaked little gypsy girl. Or with him.

Especially when he intended to use this fake relationship with Molly to explore his very real feelings for her.

Quietly and with deliberate slowness, Julian rose to his feet, came around the table and set a hand on his brother's shoulder. Then he whispered, very mildly, but with an edge, "Stay out of this, Garrett. I don't want to hurt you, man, and I definitely don't want to hurt her. So just stay the hell out of this."

Then he grabbed his jacket, reclaimed his cool and stalked out of his office.

"I can't believe it. I really can't. I just know you're pulling my leg, Molly."

Propped up on a stool by the granite island in the Devaneys' kitchen while her sister decorated newly baked cookies, Molly focused on filing her nails, her stomach fluttering with excitement over this being her first night as Julian's fake girlfriend. She could hardly wait to see the expression on Garrett's dark, riveting face when he eventually saw them together. Hopefully, Julian would drape his arm around her shoulders in that aloof, sexy manner he had, in a way that said *she's my girl and aren't I the hottest ticket around?*

"I'm not pulling anything, I swear," Molly assured her. "You can totally call Julian and ask him."

Kate held up her spatula in the air, her auburn-red hair—the same shade as Molly's—haphazardly knotted atop her beautiful face. She exuded such raw sexiness while wearing that frilly white apron that Molly could've hated her if she didn't love her sister so utterly.

If there was one word to describe Kate Devaney, it would be *alive.* Kate thrived doing everything and anything, which explained the rocking success of her catering business; she was a killer cook with killer curves, tall and tanned and confident and fun.

The only thing Molly truly had that might surpass Kate in the looks department was her really nice bust, but then she went through so much effort to hide it, in the end it didn't amount to much of an advantage.

"Julian and *you?* Together? I just can't give credit to this. His girls are always so—"

"Don't say it or I'll hate you," Molly grumbled, smacking her nail file down.

Kate sighed, scooped up cookies from the baking sheet and began packaging them in single decorative cellophane wraps. "Fine. I won't say it. But you know what I mean, don't you?"

Molly stood and went to look at herself in the mirror by the foyer, trying not to remember how Julian's words had hurt her yesterday morning. "You're right, I know they don't look like me," she said as she ambled back with an expression of total displeasure on her face. "They're tall and sexy and sophisticated." *But I don't care because I don't want Julian, I want Garrett,* she reminded herself.

Her lips still burned with the memory of his scorching

kiss, the incredibly sexy rumble of him growling against her mouth, as if Molly's lips were something to suckle on and bite on and feast on…

Everything inside her turned hot, and Molly shook the images aside.

Kate looked at Molly and burst out laughing. "You've really fallen for him, haven't you? I love Julian, Molls, but even I admit that whoever marries him is a fool. And I don't want *you* to be that fool, Moo."

Molly was about to assure her she would never be so stupid as to fall for Julian John. She had never seen a man so determined to sleep with so many women in her life. It was as if he had an itch he needed to get scratched and none of them seemed to cut it for him. She was about to express all of this to Kate, but then she remembered she was *supposed* to be his girlfriend already—or yeah, his *lover,* since Julian was too worldly to have girlfriends—so she clamped her mouth shut and privately thanked her lucky stars that she truly had better sense than to become notch number 1,000,340 on the mysterious and uncatchable Julian John Gage's bedpost.

Kate paused in her cookie wrapping and lifted two winged eyebrows in question. "So how did it happen? Did he just suddenly—?"

"Did I realize what a fool I've been not to finally admit little Molls is the one for me? Yeah. Exactly like that." The deep baritone that interrupted them startled Molly so much that her arms broke out in goose bumps.

She spun around as Julian shut the front door after him, and her stomach sank in mortification when she realized that once again he would find her in paint-splattered work clothes. Then she remembered she didn't care. This was Julian John and she didn't need to impress him. He al-

ready thought she looked like a by-product of a blender.
Why ruin it for him?

But it seemed wholly unfair that she would be wearing
paint marks up to her hair and he would look so clean and
male and good. Black jacket slung over his shoulder, his
burgundy Gucci tie almost undone, he looked sexily tousled and delicious. Not that Molly wanted a bite of him or
anything, but she supposed another woman would. Hell,
they all did.

But Molly had common sense in regards to him.

She mentally patted herself on the back once more while
Julian stalked forward as if he owned the place, wearing
that playful grin he'd given her ever since they were kids.

"Whatever Kate has said about me, Mopey, don't believe her. It's all due to the fact that she wanted me first."
His strong arms coiled like a steel vise around her waist
while that Beckham-blond head dipped toward hers.

Molly didn't see it coming. He moved too fast and had
incredible strength, and she was only five feet tall and
easily handled. Before she could even realize what was
happening, Julian had already reeled her in, crushing her
breasts against his rock-hard pecs as his mouth settled
firmly over hers, expertly, perfectly, oh so hotly.

And ooh. *Oooh.* A tiny working part of her mind frantically screamed at her to push him away. The only one
she should be kissing now was Garrett! But the fact was,
Julian kissed like his brother. Except Julian tasted clean
and minty and not of wine, and he kissed her as if he had
all the time in the world.

Those silken playboy's lips pressed with painstaking
gentleness against hers and moved so languorously that all
her senses began to spin out of control. Molly became mag-
netized. *Hypnotized.* Almost transported to the night her

entire world had flipped upside down, and she'd glanced down to find her heart had been stolen from her chest.

She wasn't even sure she was standing anymore, but trusted that Julian would always catch her fall. The sudden desperate urge to press closer to him flitted through her, burned through her being as he lingered in his kiss for a thrilling, electrifying second, and then he was gone. Leaving her dazed and surprised and scatterbrained as he set her away—thankfully keeping a steady hand on her elbow until she found her ground.

He said something once it was over. She thought it was hello.

Molly pushed her hair back, feeling dazed. "Uh—hi."

He asked her something, his voice huskier than usual, his eyes at half-mast, and she stared at his mouth. His soft yet strong lips became the center of her attention, for she wondered what exactly it was about those lips that had felt so incredibly good when he'd put them on hers.

Even her knees had taken a hit.

She fought to calm down, but remained so shaken she ended up snapping at him for catching her unaware. "What are you doing here, JJ?" she asked, glaring, using his old kiddie nickname just to punish him.

Julian remained aloof and calmly popped a cookie straight from the baking sheet into his mouth. "Nothing, pumpkin buns. Just wanted to check in on my girl." He strode over and squeezed her butt, whispering only for her ears, "JJ? You're going to pay for that, Molls."

She fake giggled so Kate wouldn't notice anything strange and pulled away, her buttocks aflame from his touch. How to get back at him? She said the first thing that came to mind when she caught Kate's confused expression. "JJ loves for me to call him all sorts of pet names when we're...you know," she told her.

"JJ?" Kate turned to Julian, hands on hips, spatula held like a sword. "I thought you absolutely loathed that nickname."

Julian shot Molly a warning look. "I do," he said, jaw square as a cutting board. "But little Molls calls me JJ exclusively when she wants me to spank her."

Molly's satisfaction in getting back at him vanished.

Her cheeks burst into flames. She wanted to die of embarrassment, for now her sister would forever believe her to be into that kind of kinky stuff.

"Baby, its barely afternoon and I still need to make myself sexy and sophisticated for you," she told him as she went around the kitchen and shot him a scowl from behind Kate's shoulders. "Not all of us come by it naturally. Now you'll have to wait for me a bit. I'm sure Kate and her spatula would love to keep you company, though."

He moved fluidly, nonplussed. "I have a better idea, bun-buns. Why don't I help you get dressed, hmm?" Before Molly could deny him, he'd followed her into her bedroom and locked them inside while Kate remained in the kitchen, no doubt still wide-eyed.

"Will you *puleeze* stop provoking me," Molly hissed, pushing him against the door. "Stop calling me bun-buns."

He leaned forward with gritted teeth. "Who's provoking who? You know I freaking hate JJ!"

"And don't you dare kiss me again without warning like you just did!"

"If you ever call me JJ again, I'm going to kiss you—with tongue. So *don't,* otherwise I'll think you *want* my tongue inside your mouth!"

He glared at her and she glared back, wishing that a stream of butterflies hadn't just migrated to her stomach. She couldn't help but wonder what Julian did with his loathed tongue that drove all women crazy, crazy, *crazy*….

"Are we clear about this, Molls?" he demanded, using his thumb and forefinger to tip her head back and force her to meet his gaze. She was appalled to realize she had apparently been staring dumbly at his mouth.

She nodded so that he would release her and swallowed, some rebel inside her wanting to test him and say: *Yes, JJ.*

Then she groaned and thrust him away. "Why, oh, why did you have to tell her you spanked me?" She shook her head and rubbed her temples in complete mortification.

"Because sometimes I swear to God you want me to." He swatted her butt and strolled to the closet, leaving her to grapple with incredibly strange and powerful emotions and an uncomfortably stinging butt.

"So." He yanked out a huge suitcase, turned back and cocked a devilish eyebrow at her. "I told the love of your life that you were moving in with me. What do you say about that, my little Picasso?"

"Was he jealous?"

That smile again. "About as close to banging his head on a wall as I've seen him."

Molly yanked her panty drawer open. "Then I'd be delighted."

Three

"So what else did the love of my life say?" Molly asked as they made a pit stop for food on their way back to Julian's place. He was always hungry. It seemed that his muscles needed a lot of glucose, all the time. The man had a friends group for every sport he participated in: soccer, basketball, kayaks, zip-lining, even the more extreme hang-gliding gigs.

Those hard, taut muscles on his arms and legs and abs and the magnificent golden hue of his skin obviously didn't come from being in an office all day.

He was so lean, he could probably tackle a decathlon as easily as he tackled women in bed.... Hmm, she wondered if Garrett would soon tackle *her* in bed.

"Wait here," he said as he slid his silver Aston Martin into the only vacant parking slot in front of a frozen yogurt chain.

"Hey will you get me an Oreo milk shake with—"

"Three cherries on top—one for chewing, one for sucking and one to leave at the bottom?"

Molly grinned and nodded, and she could still hear his rumbling chuckle even after he'd closed the door.

Minutes later, he returned, and she found herself scowling down at her milk shake. "Why is there a phone number written on my milk shake cup?"

With an easy flick of his wrist, he turned the key and his car engine roared back to life.

"Julian!"

He flung his hands up in exasperation. "I didn't ask for it, Molls."

She shook her head in distaste. But then, could she blame the cashier or whoever had scrambled to write her hopes on Molly's milk shake? Julian was graced with both a face and body that made women gape, stammer and stutter—then behave like twits. That was a fact. And there was nothing Molly—or even Julian—could do about it.

Still, it rankled, and Molly kept shaking her head. "Honestly. I have no idea who in their right mind would hook up with you."

He shifted sideways and put the car in Reverse, then reached out and chucked her chin. "Apparently *you*."

Molly laughed and started chewing her first cherry. "You haven't told me what the love of my life has to say about me—his one true love—hanging out with the likes of you."

Julian turned the wheel, shifted gears and sped onto the highway. "He mentioned guns. At dawn."

Molly sucked on her second cherry. "Just please don't make me a widow before I even marry him."

"*Marry*. Whoa. Now there's a big word."

"There's nothing wrong with the word *marriage*."

"I said it was a big word."

She stopped sucking on her cherry and stared at him in suspicion, pushing the cherry to one side of her mouth as she talked. "And please don't tell me when you said guns you were talking about your biceps again?"

He just smiled that sexy smile. As if he knew a secret Molly didn't. Or as if he'd seen her naked without her knowledge. *Oops, where did that thought come from?*

Her stomach jittered all of a sudden, and she figured she might be cold. It had started raining when they loaded up her suitcases, and now her clothes were soaked and clinging to her skin. Which was unfortunate, because she'd changed into something Julian might even consider sexy and sophisticated. Not because she cared what he thought, but just to prove to him that Molly Devaney had money of her own, had success on her own and only dressed comfortably because she believed inner beauty was more important than material stuff.

Now as she contemplated her soggy outfit, she didn't know if her goose bumps were due to her wet tank or the cold milk shake or excitement.

Julian became pensive as he drove, but that was fine with her. Molly chattered on in her excitement about how she was going to get Garrett, how she could use one of Julian's spare bedrooms if she felt suddenly inspired and had to paint… She *did* have an exhibition soon and needed to finish two more pieces within the next month.

When they arrived at his apartment building, he asked her if he could show her something and Molly nodded eagerly. Eduardo, one of the doormen, took charge of delivering her bags to the twelfth floor while Julian guided her to another elevator and pressed P. They were carried up to the penthouse.

What greeted them when the elevator doors opened was an enormous white space, with floor-to-ceiling windows in every corner and the smell of fresh paint lingering in the air.

"Wow. What is this?"

He met her gaze, and she was mesmerized by the proud gleam in his eyes, could even hear the pride in his gruff voice. "These just so happen to be my future offices."

Molly's eyes rounded in surprise. "You—what do you mean? Is the *Daily* moving from downtown?"

The Gage family owned the most thriving and successful newspaper conglomerate in all of Texas, which included several print publications, internet news sites and some cable-TV channels, all working under the umbrella of their first paper, the *San Antonio Daily*. It was a business of three generations and one that gave the family immense wealth and untold power. Their offices occupied an entire block downtown, so Molly couldn't quite believe the move would be so easy.

A second passed before Julian answered, and it was as though he was selecting his words carefully. "No. I'm the only one moving out, Molls."

Molly stared at his somber expression, loud warning bells chiming in her head. She immediately sensed this development was not a positive thing for the family. "Do your brothers know about this, Jules?" she asked, treading cautiously.

"They will."

Molly took a couple of minutes to digest this shocking news. Her stomach did weird things at the thought of drama within the family, which had always seemed to revolve around Julian and his rebel ways. She still remembered each one of the times he'd been sent abroad for who knew what kinds of wrongdoing. Molly had missed her friend terribly, like she'd miss a thumb or an arm or a crucial and important part of her. All she remembered about those wretched months was that she'd cried. A lot.

Now she watched him move lithely across his new office area, easily stepping over plastic tarps while he surveyed the electrical wires that stuck out from the scattered pillars, and she wondered why he'd want to bail out on the family's extremely successful newspaper and publishing business.

As the head of PR and chief of advertising for the company, Julian had the best part of the pie, in her humble opinion. He had the same whopping salary, just as many shares in the company as his brothers but the fewest responsibilities, which allowed him to have the most fun, the most women and the most time for hobbies like flying that Cessna plane he so loved and doing all the sports he enjoyed. Why would he leave the *San Antonio Daily?*

"I had no idea you were unhappy where you were," she said as she caught up with him, searching his face.

He stared out the wide windows and the sunlight caught a dozen golden flecks in his green eyes. "I'm dissatisfied with my life, though not necessarily unhappy. A change was in order."

Her heart clenched with a strange emotion; she supposed it might be disappointment, for she'd believed they were close enough for him to share this important information with her sooner. As in, before he signed the lease for the penthouse. But then Julian was very reserved with his emotions, which was why people thought he had none. "So…" She walked through the space with him, taking in each new desk waiting for its worker. "How long have you been planning this?"

She wanted to know more but also knew Julian disliked being pushed too far, and she sensed that this was all she would get for now.

"A couple of years. Maybe my whole life."

He smiled down at her, a truly honest and content smile, and captivated by it, she returned it in kind, was helpless not to. But while a part of her wanted to clap and say *good for you!* there was another part, the one that was also loyal to the entire Gage family, that wished he'd reconsider. For Molly's entire life, she'd sided with Julian about everything, anytime and anywhere, yet now she felt torn. Because she'd given her heart to Garrett two weeks ago and knew for certain that she'd never get it back. And she knew Garrett would fight tooth and claw to keep Julian in the business.

He was one of their greatest assets and the only Gage brother cocky enough to neither worry nor care about appearances. His suave manner and mysterious ways seemed to both annoy and charm the competition, and made him the best PR person in the state. Molly doubted the *Daily* would have even half the amount of advertisers it did when Julian no longer had a hand in reeling them in. Maybe he would reconsider in due time?

Continuing their stroll with a sigh, she nearly bumped into a blank wall. "All this white space could use something, you know," she suddenly said aloud.

From a few feet away, Julian chuckled, and the husky sound created a compelling echo in the wide-open room. "Now, why did I know you were going to say that?" he asked as he came over.

She grinned and wrinkled her nose at him. "Maybe because I don't like blank walls and you've known this for twenty years or more."

Stopping just an arm's length away, he smoothed the wrinkle in her nose with one lone fingertip. "Then make a mural for me. This entire wall—make it yours."

Molly held his penetrating stare, her nose itching where

he'd touched it. As the wheels in her head started spinning, she turned to the wall and found that her muse had already jumped with an idea. "Are you high? My individual paintings already command five-figure prices. A mural would run at least 150,000 and it would take me months. I need to talk to my gallerist."

Her gallerist had once represented Warhol and he was the savviest art dealer around, selling the craziest, most daring and contemporary art in the world. He was also Julian's friend.

"Leave Blackstone out of it. A hundred and fifty it is."

She gasped. "Jules, I can't charge you that, it feels like I'm robbing my best friend."

"Then it should be fun. A hundred-fifty K, Molls, but make it real pretty for me. As pretty as you." His smile flashed charmingly, and a bucket of excitement settled in Molly's stomach until she could hardly stand it. She didn't know if it was due to the fabulous deal she'd just closed or to being called pretty for once without it being accompanied by an insult to her clothes attached. Perhaps it was both.

"Of course, Jules!" Pulling herself up by grabbing onto the collar of his shirt, she quickly kissed his hard jaw, then wished she hadn't, because he totally stiffened. "Thanks. When can I start?"

He spun for the elevator and cranked his neck as though it had cramped on him. "Tomorrow if you'd like," he said.

Molly floated in a cloud of bliss as she followed him. Had she really just landed an enormous work space just upstairs for the time being?

Had she just been commissioned for her first *mural?*

She could hardly believe her good fortune, although she'd always enjoyed a certain share of luck when it came to her art. The sudden interest from a top New York gallery a couple of years before had placed her works in several important collectors' homes, and before she knew it her name was being piled up next to contemporary artists like David Salle and Sean Scully; big, big, *big* names in the art world. Now for the first time in her twenty-three years, maybe some of that creative luck would rub off on her sadly lacking love life. Maybe she was close to getting what she wanted with Garrett.

Thanks to Julian, for sure.

Because she'd suddenly realized that, just as her canvases did not miraculously paint themselves, her love life wouldn't happen without some encouragement. And that was where Julian's help making Garrett jealous fit in.

Once back in Julian's spacious apartment, Molly chose the guest bedroom to the left of his room, a space done in a pastel blue-and-green palette that she'd always found soothing. She retrieved her night creams, day creams, moisturizing creams, shampoos and toothbrush and aligned them all on the sink, then peeled out of her still-damp clothes, showered and slipped into her sleep shirt, which was actually an old T-shirt Julian had used in high school and his mother had sent to the Donation Station. Nobody knew Molly had fished this shirt out of the garbage bag for being the softest and most worn, and Julian would hardly remember he'd ever owned it.

Once ready for bed, she went out in the hall to look for him and hoped to propose they watch a movie, but his bedroom door was closed. Disappointment crept in, so then she went to bed and lay there, gazing at the walls, the curtains and the ceiling fan for hours.

Sleep eluded her, and her thoughts kept drifting toward Garrett. His black hair, those onyx eyes with the sooty lashes, and *oh, God,* the way he'd kissed her two weeks ago. She remembered that kiss so perfectly that she'd been reliving it nightly, in bed, as she futilely tried to fall asleep.

"I think I'd like to be a spinster," Molly had told Kate that evening as they stood out on the terrace of the Gage mansion, gazing into the brightly lit masquerade party transpiring inside the sprawling 10,000-square-foot home.

Kate had obviously laughed. "Molls. Why on earth would you say that?" She'd lovingly tousled her hair, which Molly had worn loose for the evening. "You're beautiful and sweet and any man would be lucky to have you."

"It's just that no man seems to live up to my expectations."

With a dreary sigh, Molly showed Kate the picture of the three Gage brothers she carried in her iPhone. It featured the gray-eyed, responsible Landon, the dark-haired, honorable Garrett and of course the sex god playboy, Julian. As her favorite Gage brother, Julian was everything that a good husband was *not*.

"I know what you mean," Kate said softly, staring longingly at the picture.

It couldn't have been easy for her to play both mother and father to Molly while she herself had been barely a teen. Although Eleanor Gage had been a stand-in mother for both of them, she was a stern woman, and as one did when running on survival instincts, both girls had tried to put on their best behavior and their whitest smiles with the person who'd given them food and shelter. But when alone, Molly would seek out Kate's warmth and support like she'd seek out a pillow and blanket. Especially during those lonely times when Julian had been sent away. Sometimes Molly even wondered if she wasn't to blame for Kate's lack of a love life, a husband and a family of her own. The thought made her stomach feel heavy.

"You deserve someone, too," Molly whispered.

Kate smiled brightly and winked at her. "Then let's go find one," she teased and rushed for the double doors that led inside, but Molly groaned and stayed back, loathing her stupid costume.

She had been dared by Julian to dress as a tavern wench tonight. And of course he knew Molly could never ignore a dare that he delivered. Alas, now here she was. In an outfit so tight she was barely able to breathe, which showcased her breasts in a way that made her feel as if she'd just stepped out of a porn magazine.

She had never felt so exposed in her life, and as soon as she saw Julian, probably dressed like some evil creature, for sure, Molly was going to tell him off for being such a cad. "I'll catch up in a sec," she lied to Kate before her sister disappeared inside.

Instead of following, she edged farther out on the terrace, where it was dark and the air was fresh from the gardens and nobody would see her in her corseted wench costume.

A silhouette by the banister caught her attention.

Someone was coming toward her. Zorro? she wondered. Or was it the Phantom of the Opera? Or maybe it was Westley, the dangerously sexy man from Molly's favorite movie, *The Princess Bride.*

Whoever he was, he was hot. Clad all in black: black cape, a cloth mask covering both his hair and the upper part of his face. Black boots. And that smile. It just had to be Julian. Nobody smiled like Julian. He smiled like a wolf and made you want to be the lamb he was going to eat; it was very, very bizarre how he pulled that off.

She suddenly caught his glimmering eyes straying to her prominent cleavage and she felt something hot coil inside her belly.

"Well, well, well…" he murmured as he continued to approach.

His voice was thick and slurred, and she wondered how much he'd drunk tonight. He didn't sound like himself at all.

He smiled again and her stomach tightened under his appreciation.

He had a drink in his hand, and when he raised it to his lips, watching her with those eerily sparkling eyes, she noticed that his glass was empty. He cursed under his breath, shook his head and swung around to leave, murmuring something about being crazy.

She frowned when she realized she would not be getting to tell him off just yet. "You're going to leave me all alone out here?" she playfully called after him.

He paused for a moment, then turned, set the cup aside, and started for her with sudden purpose. With each long, determined stride, he dived deeper into the shadows Molly had been trying to hide herself in.

He was not smiling now. Something in his approach, in the tension in his shoulders, made her heart begin to pound. And pound faster. Faster. The way he moved, the way he frightened her…

It couldn't possibly, possibly, be Julian.

She began, "What—?"

He pulled her up against him, so fast that her lips flew open and she sucked in a shocked mouthful of air. In one fluid move, he pinned her hands at her sides, then bent his face to hers, mask to mask. Molly had stopped breathing.

It was too dark to make out this stranger's eye color, but she could still sense that gaze like a laser beam boring into her being. Her heart faltered when he made a sound, low and completely unrecognizable—a rumbling groan that was so hot and so male her toes curled.

His lips touched hers. The lightest of touches. Just a graze. Like the tiny spark that sets loose a wildfire. And Molly exploded with a rush of wanting so powerful it scorched every inch of her insides, infusing every particle of her being with heat.

Her lips opened as though on their own, and her body melted under his as a strange, embarrassing little moan escaped her. He seemed to like it, for his answering growl vibrated in her mouth as his lips latched firmly over hers.

He kissed her so possessively, a tornado of pleasure shot through her veins and her heartbeat skyrocketed to the ozone layer. His fingers bit into her buttocks as he dragged her up against him. Closer. Closest. Thrusting his tongue into her mouth with a groan of pleasure.

She tasted wine and immediately felt drunk on him. High on him. Wild for him. She was lost to a staggering rush of sensations as their mouths devoured each other with wet, greedy licks and suckles, her skin screaming with delicious agony as his hand stroked up her arms, caressing her. She had never felt so alive, so connected to another human being, as though her body were an extension of his larger, stronger one.

It was like being caught in a deluge of rain, and now she could feel his desire pour over her. Swimming in sensations, she felt the warm metal of a ring sliding upward as he stroked her shoulders, and her eyes jerked open when she realized this man kissing her, this man was…

Garrett?

How could it be?

He rarely put so much as a finger on her, he was so protective. Julian was always pawing her and she loved the little ways his touch made her feel. But while Garrett rarely reached out for her, when he did, Molly always felt this thick, smooth ring anywhere he put his hand. When he grasped her hand in his—ring. When he petted the top of her head—ring. When he secured her elbow to keep her from falling—aha. Ring.

Now Garrett was kissing her as if he was eating her alive, his ring almost like a brand across her skin as his hand greedily stroked her shoulders, then suddenly her throat, down her collarbone, to the top swell of her breast, tracing the shape of her.

He mumbled something, but she could hardly hear him through the roaring of her own heartbeat, his voice sounding alien and lust-roughened as he fiercely bent down to lick the exposed skin.

Rocked with the realization that this man, untouchable to her like all the Gages had been for her entire life, had thrown all caution to the wind and was kissing her as if his life depended on it left her knees in such a weakened state that she clung to him even while she tried to edge back to steal a quick peek at his ring.

The platinum band glinted in the shadows as he fondled her breasts, and yes, it was the same one-of-a-kind ring Garrett always wore, with a blue diamond at its center.

It *was* Garrett fondling her shamelessly.

And it felt so good, his touch so arousing, a rush of liquid heat flooded her between her thighs.

He groaned in misery when she went still with shock, yet he pulled her tighter against him anyway, as though her lips were powerful magnets for his. "Shh," she heard him say, cooing to her, calming her as if she were both precious and wild. "Shh…"

When he edged his knee between her legs to part them, the skirt of her dress rose, and he expertly eased his hand through the layers of fabric to cup her between her legs, right where she'd grown wet for him. The heat of his palm burned through her panties, and her bones seemed to disintegrate into nothing. Nothing but heat and pleasure and sensation.

"Oh," she gasped, body tensing as his fingers began stroking in slow, lazy circles, her head exploding in disbelief and excitement as a rush of hot lightning coursed through her.

His touch consumed her.

He touched her as if he owned her. As if he *knew* and *cherished* everything about her.

She'd never known she could respond like this to another human being.

She'd tried never to feel anything romantic for any of these Gage men—because they were her protectors and Kate said they were like their brothers and were therefore unavailable. But this one...this one wanted her and clearly didn't give one whit about what Kate said. What anyone said. And Molly hadn't realized she wanted him back so much until this very moment, when she was melting in his arms in a way she had never, ever imagined.

Needy sounds bubbled up in her throat as she rocked her hips against him, helpless to stop herself, her body a puppet to masterful hands that continued expertly stroking her. The sensations were so powerful she whimpered in mingled fear and longing, her insides coiling tightly like springs.

He groaned and bent his head to her ear, biting the lobe hungrily, desperately, those gut-wrenchingly sexy noises from his throat shooting arrows of heat to her nerve endings. His hungry mouth traveled all over her neck, leaving a wet path that sizzled as he pressed the heel of his palm seductively between her legs, rubbing and stroking exactly the parts that most ached and hurt and burned.

And then the worst part was that, with one more expert touch, one firm press with the heel of his hand, she'd exploded.

Molly still remembered the way she had trembled with that touch alone, and then she had wanted to cry, because she'd never had an orgasm before. Embarrassed to her core, she'd pushed him away as soon as she was able and gritted, "Don't touch me. Don't even talk to me! This never happened—never!"

And she'd yanked off her stupid mask, flung it aside and left.

The next day, Garrett had pretended that nothing happened, just as she'd told him to. And when she'd gone to talk to Julian about it, he'd been too hung over to focus and in a pissy mood. So she'd kept it to herself for over a dozen nights, her sexual siren having been awakened, now hungry for more and determined to do something about it. Once again, Molly wanted to weep in her bed in silence.

She wished she hadn't kissed him.

She wished she hadn't stopped.

She wished she hadn't pushed him away.

She wished she'd had the courage to face the music, so that he would have done the same.

But more than anything, she wished to feel again like she'd felt that night.

Garrett had broken down and revealed his feelings for her in an unmistakable way, and though Molly had gloried in his intimate touch and his incredible kiss, she'd gotten scared in the end.

She wished she hadn't given out the message that she wasn't receptive to more of his delicious kisses and touches. Because the more she thought of and relived that kiss, the more she was convinced that unique connection wasn't typical and that she'd just found her *soul mate*.

Without words, she'd been able to feel his love so powerfully that her own heart had sung inside her chest, and she ached desperately to be with him again.

Swallowing back a lump in her throat, she pounded the pillow and shifted to lie facedown on the bed. *Go to sleep, Molly, and tomorrow you can show Garrett what he's missing.*

But rather than give her comfort, the thought only made her realize that the one person who had been missing out on the best things in life was Molly.

Julian knew exactly why he couldn't sleep, why he was feeling so cranky and why everything felt like crap lately.

It was all Molly Devaney's fault.

She was driving him crazy in every possible way he could imagine.

First with the Garrett thing. And now just thinking about her sleeping next door made him toss restlessly in bed, frustrated beyond measure.

Tonight, it had been raining outside when they loaded up her suitcases. By the time Molly had stepped into his apartment, she'd looked so…wet. God, he'd really tried not to look at the way she needed to peel her shirt back from her breasts, but he lacked the willpower.

Lying back in his bed, he tried to cool down his roiling blood, his head swimming with the sight of her breasts, perfectly round, with those pointy nipples straining against the fabric of her top.

And when she'd kissed him upstairs, so happy to be painting the mural for him, it had taken all his willpower not to turn his face and capture that kiss with his lips, kiss her long and hard as if he'd wanted to back in her apartment—where she'd been flushed and gasping for breath after the silly little peck he'd given her. And those cherries. Goddamn the sounds she made as she ate those miserable cherries!

It had been a miracle Julian hadn't lunged across the seat of his car, taken her face between his hands and suckled each and every cherry from her cool and sassy mouth.

Hell, this is the worst idea I've ever had in my life.

For years, Julian had grown up with rules that he'd tried to follow, knowing the only girl he'd ever respected and admired was out of his reach. Molly was the one woman Julian would want to be locked in a closet with. Stranded on a deserted island with. She was the only good and pure thing in his life, and despite some failed efforts, he'd tried to keep it that way. Unsullied and unsoiled, happy and protected.

Growing up, he'd always imagined they would have each other. Molly had never liked to date, and she'd always needed Julian. Julian had kept his hands off her and *on* just about anyone else in his efforts to keep busy, stay focused and more importantly, stay away from Molly.

But now—she wanted Garrett.

A Gage.

Julian's stomach roiled with nausea at the reminder. God. He'd never imagined this could ever happen.

At first, he'd thought she was pulling his leg, or trying to make *him* jealous. In the back of his mind, he'd always imagined that if Molly ever fell in love with one of the Gage brothers, it would be…him. Dammit, him and *only* him. Because she sure as hell never seemed to look at anyone else.

Even his family had thought Molly wanted him, which was why every time he got close to Molly, all hell would break loose. His mother, Landon, Garrett, even Kate would pounce. Julian had suffered endless lectures from them all about being good to Molly, staying away from Molly, respecting Molly or finding another home. For the most part, he had been good. Really good.

But now, years and what felt like aeons later, the fact that Molly wanted his brother was a game changer. Julian had been living in this hell long enough, and he could no longer kid himself that the magic, the pull, the impossible chemistry between Molly and him was only due to friendship. He knew full well that when she made his groin throb with her smiles, they were not friendly feelings. Much less brotherly ones.

He'd been dreaming about her for *years*. Powerful dreams. Sexual dreams. Dreams that left him drenched in sweat and groaning in pain and reaching for the first pair of female legs that passed him.

Yeah, he'd thought if he'd had sex more often, his powerful reactions to her would diminish. But all it did was make him want her more—because none of those women were Molly.

No. *No one* could ever even compare to that effervescent little bombshell—no one.

Now he just needed to play his game right. Julian might have a long comfortable fuse where his temper was concerned, but when it came to Molly, his fuse had run damn short. If she kept this up he was going to do something reckless and stupid.

And he didn't want to be reckless and stupid.

He'd been moving his pieces all in the direction of one goal so he could stake his claim on her once and for all.

Now he'd prove to his family that he did not need them, and that he would never hurt a single hair on Molly's beautiful head. He needed them to see that he was worthy of her, that he wanted her for real and not just for sex—though of course when that happened, it was going to be damned amazing, too. But more importantly, he needed to show them that he would do whatever it took to have her. Even cut his ties with them *all*.

If Molly was ever going to settle down with a guy, she was settling down with Julian. Whether they liked it or not.

And as for Molly...

He had to make her see that *he* was the man for her and always had been—and once and for all, he had to finish what he'd started the night he'd kissed her heart out at the masquerade party.

Four

Something about sleeping in Julian's apartment made Molly restless.

Well past midnight, still tortured by the memory of Garrett's kiss, she found herself tiptoeing down the hall toward the kitchen in the hopes of finding some sort of sleep aid in his cupboards. She had her heart set on Sleepytime Tea, but valerian root or chamomile would do, too. Hey, at this point, she'd take anything as long as it meant quieting her troubled brain and getting some rest.

But what she found on her way to the cupboards was a beautifully sculpted, seminaked man instead—and the sight of him was sure to give her permanent insomnia.

Wearing only a pair of white cotton briefs that hugged his buttocks perfectly, he leaned against the open refrigerator door, his head stuck inside as he surveyed the food.

Molly stopped in her tracks, her heart flying to her throat.

The warm fridge light silhouetted Julian's magnificent form, shamelessly caressing every dent, every shadow and every sharp rise of lean, ripped muscle. Her breasts pricked unexpectedly. And suddenly he was not just Julian.

He was every inch…Julian John Gage.

Sexy playboy, dangerous male.

Not a hero, not harmless and definitely not just a friend.

A tremor rushed down her legs as her eyes helplessly drank up what was so blatantly on display, aided by the moonlight that filtered through the windows; she took in the sinewy arm folded above his head as he leaned forward, the broad muscled back, the lean hips and…the rest. His long, muscled calves and hamstrings, his hard buttocks under that snug white cotton.

Her temperature skyrocketed. Not because he was utterly sexy in a way that made her want to swim in ice right now, but because she was here. With him. At midnight. And he was about 90 percent *naked*. When it should be Garrett here, Garrett almost naked, Garrett in her head.

Her hormones clearly knew nothing of reason. They burst into action until she could feel the hot little pinpricks all over her body, to her utter confusion and despair.

Even her fingers tingled at her sides with a painful itch to trace the muscles on his back, determine the texture, the hardness, paint the thick ropes straining in his forearms. For a wild moment she kidded herself that it was the artist in her; it had to be. For she felt the same fever she did when she was gripped with the need to paint.

Except now she was gripped with the need to trace the length of Julian John.

With finger paint. All of him. She thought wildly that if he were a canvas, she would not leave an inch of him unpainted except his lips. He was just too masculine to wear them any way but bare.

But she could still trace them with her fingertips and find out what sort of power they held when they kissed her. She could explore the thick bottom one and then the top one and she might even kiss them again just to be sure her memory wasn't failing her...

Molly, you love Garrett, you tramp!

Shocked by the untoward thoughts, she snapped back to the present and swallowed a lump in her throat. An awful guilt surfaced inside her. Had she actually been thinking of accosting Julian in his own kitchen? What was wrong with her?

Ever since that evening at the masquerade, it felt as if her entire life had been flipped over as easily as a pancake.

Now she could not stop thinking about kissing, touching, tasting, wanting. Garrett had awakened the desperate needs of a woman inside her, and Molly felt so hyperaware of her body now, even her reactions to Julian were uncommonly, embarrassingly...unsettling.

See what you've done to me, Garrett? Apparently I'm a nymphomaniac now.

"Um. Did you forget you have a guest here?" she blurted out from her spot a few feet away.

Julian's shoulders stiffened almost imperceptibly. His head dropped an inch or so, that gorgeous mane with sun-streaked strands that were lighter than the others. "Damn—you're supposed to be asleep, Molls." He pulled his head out of the fridge, his chin dropping an inch or so as he faced her, his hair catching the light just right.

"People with insomnia don't sleep, Jules."

Molly should go back to her bedroom, she supposed, but being squeamish about a man's near-nakedness did not go with her artistic persona. She had to treat it as a natural state of being, or at least that was what she told herself as she woodenly walked over and opened and shut cabinet doors in search of her tea.

"Here, have some milk, always works for me." He shoved the carton he'd just drunk from in her direction.

Molly took it and set her lips over the place his mouth had been, trying not to get too hooked on that discomforting detail as she downed a big gulp. Swallowing, she said, "Ah, it's cold," and handed it back, all her efforts focused solely on not noticing how velvety smooth and hairless his massive chest was.

She had never felt five feet tall when she was with Julian until today. When he seemed to hulk over her, appearing for the first time in her life almost…threatening. Extremely male.

"I'm going back to bed," he said, shoving the milk back into the fridge and shutting the door.

"Can I come sleep with you?" Molly blurted out to his retreating back.

Suddenly she just knew if she went back to sleep alone in her room, she would be haunted. By her masked man. And by Julian in sexy white cotton briefs. She desperately wanted to watch a movie with him and snuggle and sleep and get her best friend back. She ached for him to make her feel…safe. Like when they were kids.

"No," he answered without a single backward glance.

"Don't be a jackass, Jules."

"I don't sleep with women I can't take to bed," he yelled back.

"I'm not women. I'm just *me*."

"Precisely."

She scowled and said, "Just put some pants on and I'll bring my pillow. Come on, don't be mean."

She heard silence, then receding footsteps down the hall.

"Julian?" she called back tentatively.

His laugh made her hope for a moment, but then he spoke. "Good night, Molls!"

And so Molly cursed him all the way to her room, climbed alone into her bed and didn't sleep a wink.

She didn't fare so well on the second night, or on the third, either. Even though she tried every night to get him to invite her for a sleepover, the man's will was iron. She was surprised she couldn't bend him to her plea at all, but she was more surprised by the amount of effort Garrett had been putting into stopping her from getting into a "relationship" with Julian. Which amounted to zero so far.

That was not the approach of a man in love!

Then again, Garrett had always been the most hard-headed of the three, so he'd probably need extra incentives in order to react to her provocations.

Molly fantasized about the sexy clothing she could wear to catch his attention. She was growing so desperate, she even imagined pulling out that stupid wench costume again—but what sane person wore that? Nobody, that was who. Only Molly Devaney on a *dare* from *Julian*.

By the sixth night and seventh morning at Julian's, Molly decided she was being tortured. Cranky from lack of sleep and out of sorts from painting all night, she began to wonder if she might have taken too deep of a plunge into this whole "relationship." She'd barely even seen Garrett, much less talked to him, yet oh, boy, she'd been seeing plenty of Julian John.

Of course seeing him seminaked in the kitchen that first night took the gold.

But the close silver went to the times when he had breakfast in those linen drawstring pants that drove her crazy. He had several in different colors, and when the sunlight hit them at just the right angle, she could almost see through them. It was torture trying *not* to.

Like having an open chocolate bar stare back at you for hours and trying not to eat it. It was *crazy*.

And then watching all those bare shoulders and biceps and triceps and lats and traps and pecs and all that hairless tanned skin moving and flexing as he had breakfast nearly catapulted her to internal combustion. He was just too…defined. His virility too overwhelming to endure when she'd had no sleep.

But on the other hand, the bantering between them was wonderful.

Julian usually read the paper while Molly eyed all the junk mail, and this morning he'd accused her of being the only person he knew who actually enjoyed reading it. They'd laughed about that, among other stuff. And yet there were also moments that felt…serious. Too serious.

Every time Molly rose for more coffee, she caught Julian staring at her bare legs that peeked from under her long T-shirt. She had never in her life been more self-conscious of her walk until she came back to the table with his smooth green eyes admiring her every step. To cover up her awkwardness, she'd blurt out a silly question and Julian would jerk his gaze back to her face, asking a distracted, "What?" as if he had not even heard her.

It was not like him at all; he was usually as sharp as a tack.

Today, his teasing had continued as he drove her to her old place. Once again he mentioned her clothes. But this time his remarks had felt strangely…intimate.

He didn't exactly say her flowered sundress came from her "blender" collection, he merely said, eyes glinting in mirth, "You almost look naked without a single paint mark on you."

Naked.

Molly still wondered why her stomach had twisted like a pretzel at the word, but just the prospect of him seeing her naked made her head spin wildly. Now she waved goodbye to Julian from her front door as his Aston Martin rolled around the curve, a dazed smile lingering on her lips.

She'd promised to catch a ride home with Kate later today, once she managed to pack more of her paint supplies and found herself a dress to wear to tonight's event, a small housewarming for Landon and his wife, Beth. Although the couple had been married for two years, they'd never really taken the time to honeymoon until now. At first, they'd married because it suited Landon's business purposes and would help Beth could regain custody of her son, David. But soon they'd fallen madly in love. Now their turbulent waters had calmed and they had one of the most loving marriages Molly had ever seen.

This was the first time Julian and Molly would face all the Gages at once.

The first time they would face Garrett and make him realize he was an *idiot* for letting Molly go.

And suddenly, sexy and sophisticated wouldn't do.

Suddenly it was *crucial* that Molly look *stunning.*

Using the key neatly hidden in the potted fern outside her door, she quickly entered the apartment to the aroma of baking: cinnamon, cardamom and every scent she associated with home.

Her heart swelled at the sight of their nice, tidy place looking cozy as usual. It was prime-time girly, scattered with lacy pillows and throws on the couches and colorful accessories. Even Molly's old teddy bear sat contentedly under a Tiffany lamp.

After sequestering herself for days in an ultramasculine bachelor pad, the feminine vibe in their small one-story home appealed to her. Right then, she decided to take some of her pink pillows to Julian's place. She needed to make herself more at home if she was going to be there for a while, plus she definitely planned to stock up his cupboards with her beloved Sleepytime Tea.

"Okay, what is going on with you?"

Molly spun around to find Kate standing in the kitchen archway, her red hair tied in a ponytail, a frilly apron around her waist and a what-in-the-world expression on her face.

People used to say Kate had so much energy the sun would burn out before she did. They were right; she was always doing something.

"I just came for some more clothes. Julian's car is so impractical a kid can fit more stuff in a bike basket, I swear," Molly said.

When Kate's expression didn't soften, Molly went to the kitchen to give her a hug, which might have been easier if Kate wasn't holding a bowl.

"I can smell something's cooking, Molly. I'm like your mother and sister and father all in one."

"And *I* smell cinnamon."

Molly peeked at all the yummy offerings on the kitchen island and selected several muffins to take to Julian. She shoved them into a brown paper bag and rolled it closed with a lot of noise.

"Aww, you always do this to me," Kate said, exasperated, setting down her bowl with a plunk. "Those muffins happen to be for Landon and Beth's welcome-back party, Moo. I'll bake some for you tomorrow, okay?"

"Fine," Molly grumbled. Already halfway to her room, she retraced her path to where her sister stood and handed her the paper bag. Instead of leaving, though, she stared into eyes that were clear and blue and almost identical to hers.

Her chest felt so heavy today, she just ached to be truthful with her sister.

They'd always been close with each other. As tight as two people who were left alone in the world could possibly be. But both of them were creatively inclined and tended to disappear into their own private bubbles of imagination half the time. Molly had been known to spend months locked away, painting away her restlessness. Kate cooked her heart out as well so that by the end of the day they were both too tired to even remember that they had lives outside their jobs, jobs which also happened to be their hobbies.

Kate had always been there for Molly, a shoulder to lean on, always supportive but not suffocating. But rarely in all these years had they actually discussed men. Or the strange feelings a woman might have toward them.

It was as though they both tried to pretend men did not exist in their lives. Or maybe just pretend that, other than their wonderful relationship with the Gages, they didn't need any man *at all*.

Molly had been perfectly content with that pretense because she had Julian John's friendship. And he counted for a hundred men. So she'd never felt she lacked any male attention at all.

Until that one night, when *his brother* had made her feel *wanted*.

Until that one night when she'd been kissed and fondled until she'd burst. Literally.

Now Molly couldn't seem to stop craving that extra spark in her life. That wonderful feeling she'd felt as those hot lips, those expert hands, had reminded her she was a living, breathing woman who deserved a man's love. Because why the hell not?

But how to inform Kate of her masquerade escapade with one brother when she was now supposed to be the other's lover?

Molly just couldn't talk about Garrett yet. It was still impossible to mention that kiss that had flipped her whole life upside down. But at least she could mention something else that was gnawing at her.

"Julian hates my wardrobe," she blurted at last. She hated how her stomach cramped at the admission. And she loathed remembering how cockily Julian had assured her that this "starving artist look" would not do anything for Garrett. Damn him anyway for making her feel insecure.

Kate's eyes widened, then she cocked an I-told-you-so brow. "Now, why am I not surprised to hear that?"

"Because you've said the same. There. Does it please you, Kay? That he thinks I dress bad? Because the last thing it gives me is pleasure."

Suddenly, just remembering the sexiness of that woman she'd seen in Julian's apartment made Molly flush in anger all over again. She had to look better than *her*. She had *so* many other looks in her wardrobe, not just the "blender" ones. Jules would see.

Eyebrows joining over a nose that was dotted with freckles, Kate took a step to scrutinize Molly more closely. "Molly, I don't get you. You haven't called in days and when I text you, you tell me you're flying in Julian's airplane over to South Padre Island to get an hour of suntanning with him? Your last two unfinished paintings for the exhibit sit all alone down the hall in your studio with your deadline looming…and after years of listening to me beg you to let me give you a makeover, you finally decide to do it because of what *he* said? What is going on with you two? I couldn't sleep last night—I had to call Garrett. I'm worried sick!"

"*Garrett?* Well, what did he say?"

Looking genuinely mortified, Kate shook her ponytail and rubbed her temples. "He said to relax, that he'll talk to you. I just don't understand how this could come on so suddenly without me noticing what you two were up to. I thought this would happen later, when you were more experienced and mature."

"Forget that! Tell me what tone Garrett used. Was he angry? Concerned? Kind of possessive?"

Maybe the idiot was so arrogantly certain of Molly and her feelings for him, he thought he still had her in his grasp. Well! She'd just have to set the man straight, wouldn't she? And play harder to get with him than ever. In fact, Julian would know just how to take care of that tonight.

"I don't remember exactly what else he said, but I'm truly mortified over this. Moo, I thought you were a virgin until now?"

Kate seized her shoulders, and as her wide blue eyes searched deep into her own, Molly dropped her gaze to the floor, feeling suddenly transparent. "I *am* a virgin," she whispered, then she realized what she'd admitted to, and that the truth, right now, wouldn't do. "I mean I *was* before Jules…"

"Were you hurt your first time, Molly? Did he hurt you?"

That soft question, full of caring and concern, sent Molly for a loop. Suddenly she felt like the very red center spot of the Target sign. That was what liars felt like when they were put on the spot. So now she was going to have to draw on her imagination.

"He didn't mean to hurt me, but you know…" She trailed off and hoped to leave Kate to her own conclusion.

Which, judging by her struck expression, wasn't all that good. "I could kill him!"

"No! No! It was amazing, he was…" Helplessly hooked into an image of Julian John making love to her, Molly trailed off. Or was it Garrett she was fantasizing about? Her mouth felt so moist all of a sudden, she had to swallow. "It was actually perfect," she finished in a whisper.

"But anyway, my pride is smarting like crazy after he insulted my dress choice," she continued after a moment. "I'm truly torn, Kate. I want to show him that I can look fantastic but don't care what he thinks, either. I know you're catering for our event tonight, but do you think you can take an hour off to help make me look good?"

"Good enough to make Jules eat his words?"

"Yes!" Molly laughed, grabbing a frilly pink pillow and playfully smacking Kate with it.

She pictured Julian's face when he saw her walk through those elevator doors. Oooooh, it would be priceless. He'd look stunned and shocked and he would definitely no longer think Molly needed a new mirror.

And Garrett? He would regret every hour of these days they had been spending apart when they could have spent them together. Necking.

Kate slapped the pillow back at Molly, laughing, "Yes, I'll give you a makeover. But Molls?"

"Hmm?" Molly was already storming into her bedroom, rummaging through her closet in search of options that would make a man's mouth water. She didn't have a lot. But she still found a very nice dress in Kate's closet. She extended it to her sister, loving how the sapphire silk fabric shimmered in the light. "It has the tag on," Molly said aloud.

"Take it off," Kate said excitedly, and pulled on the plastic.

Molly shook her head. "But it's new. I can't wear this."

"Yes, you can. I was saving it for a rainy day. You'd look so lovely, Moo."

"I wish you'd stop calling me Moo. I feel like a cow." Molly hung the dress back up with a sigh, and her heart clenched for her sister. "I'll borrow this one day, but only after *you* wear it. When it rains."

They shared a smile, and minutes later, Molly found another dress in her sister's closet. It was black, fitted, and had an open back that was to die for. Molly tried it on backward and loved it so much, she decided she was doing things her own special way and cut off the label. She'd wear it this way and show plenty of cleavage tonight.

By that evening, after spending a wonderful day with Kate, getting her makeover and even helping her sister finish loading some of tonight's munchies into the catering van, Molly arrived at Julian's posh apartment building, her heart pounding in anticipation.

Her hair was held loosely by a shimmering crystal butterfly clasp, with a few soft tendrils escaping along her temples. She wasn't used to pulling her hair back, but it seemed to emphasize her features this way. Her round cheekbones, her plump lips.

Her insecurities flickered to the forefront as she asked the bellhop to hold her canvases and paints below until she rang for them. He kept staring at her as if he'd never seen her before, and she wanted to run back home and put on a boho skirt, let her hair down and grab a huge pair of earrings.

But no. This was not the time to feel insecure.

She would show Julian sexy and confident if it killed her.

She crossed the marble lobby with purpose, aware of her hips swaying, the material clinging to her skin. Garrett was going to like what she was wearing; if he'd liked the wench costume, then he would love this one for sure. And if Julian didn't like it? Her stomach did a twist inside her, and she wondered what that meant. Hopefully it meant *screw him*.

She wasn't wearing this for him. *At all*.

Taking in a deep breath, she waved at the receptionist and pushed the elevator's up button.

All right. Here goes nothing....

The elevator chimed, and Julian glanced up from the bar and almost dropped the bottle of wine he'd been examining. It was a Penfolds Grange Hermitage 1951—so rare and prized, only twenty bottles were left in the entire world, with the last having sold at auction for almost fifty thousand dollars.

But who cared about that now?

Because an exotic-looking creature resembling Molly had just stepped off the elevator, and something that felt like a paddle struck him in the chest, the gut and right between his straining eyeballs.

Holy mama.

He'd though this morning had been tough, watching that redheaded little package prance around in an old T shirt of his with those curvy bare legs begging to be stroked.

And now...

He was certain that never in his life, after dating models, actresses and even a pampered princess, had he been as fired up by the sight of a woman as he was this instant, watching Molly Devaney and her pinup body walk toward him in that minuscule black dress.

She looked like a sexpot. A sex goddess. A sex *bomb*. Awakening every Neanderthal instinct inside of him.

Julian could hardly take her all in with one long sweep of his eyes, he was so dumbstruck.

Her titian hair was drawn back into some sort of careless knot, but several soft wisps escaped to frame her lovely face, the overall look enhancing the delicacy of her doll-like features. Her lovely, heart-shaped lips shone with a peach-colored gloss, and whatever silver-gray shade of eye shadow she'd worn made her eyes look even rounder and bluer than usual. Her earrings were small pearly dots, unlike her usual flashy chandelier style, and they made her look so elegant he wanted to fly her to Monaco on his jet right now and seat her next to him at a baccarat table.

Then the dress. Ahh, the dress. The satiny black fabric fell from her nape to drape over a pair of beautiful round breasts he'd kill to taste while the plunging neckline revealed inches and inches of smooth porcelain skin in the cleavage between. The skirt was barely a couple of inches long, and it hugged her rounded hips like Lycra. Suddenly he wanted to be that skirt. That dress. That cloth that molded to her and felt her and hugged her and practically rode those curves all over the place.

Molly had always been the funniest baby, the happiest baby he'd ever seen in his life. She cackled all the time. Especially with him. Now she was entirely, 100 percent, take-me-serious woman. And Julian was primed to stop mucking around with her and ready to do some serious, serious things with her. Aww, *crap!*

This was going to be a long night.

Schooling his expression, he set the wine bottle down and noticed his hand wasn't so steady. Not while his heart was doing vaults and backflips. "Is something wrong with your usual clothes, Molls?" He was amazed his voice made it past his dry throat.

"As a matter of fact, yes." She planted her hands on her

hips, thrusting her chin up in a silent dare. "They're not sophisticated and sexy, according to you."

He cocked a brow and remained silent, mentally deliberating what in the world to do now. A part of him wanted to escort this impostor out the door and demand to know where his red-haired, paint-streaked imp was. And another part was just thinking of how good this woman would look in his bedroom. Splayed open on his bed…where he would give her a goddamned hickey that would sting like hell tomorrow…

Okay, no.

No.

He was not doing any of that.

Not so soon and not like this.

But hell, had she actually picked this dress for *Garrett?*

His jaw locked in wordless jealousy, his eyes so starved they felt like Ping-Pong balls as they went from her prominent cleavage to her narrow waist to her sexy stilettos and back to the enticing swell of her breasts and to her slim, sleek arms. A torch blazed inside his chest and the heat quickly spread to every corner of his tense body. "You call that sophisticated and sexy?" he asked gruffly.

Yeah. It was definitely sophisticated and it was so damned sexy his eyes were about to burst. But it was also practically nonexistent. And he told her so.

She stuck her little pink tongue out at him. "Eat your heart out, Jules. I look good."

He was not even going to think of all the places he wanted to feel that little tongue. Really. "*Good* is not the word I'd use."

"All right. I look amazing," Molly countered.

"Says who? You?"

"Come on, I can see you struggling, Jules. Be the better man and admit it," Molly teased, clearly enjoying this.

"I'm the only man here, Molls, and I'd gladly admit it if I wasn't so busy looking for the rest of the dress. So? Where's the rest of the goddamned dress?"

Her smile wavered. "You don't like it? Fine. I'm not wearing this to impress you." With a stiff shrug, she breezed past him to her bedroom, where she began shoving her things into a small clutch purse.

Julian followed her to the threshold of her room and watched her buttocks wiggle as she bent over. His mouth watered. She looked so sweet and so delicious he was salivating like a dog.

He'd had mile-long legs wrapped around his body, centerfold lips around his privates and breasts the size of melons in his hands. And he had never, ever, been so turned on.

He wanted Molly so bad he'd die for it.

He wanted to cup her breasts and suckle her until his jaw ached. He wanted to unpin her hair and watch as every fiery-red strand fell to caress the lovely curve of her nape and shoulders. He wanted to take a plunge into her cleavage and lick his way downward until he found the very center of her being—and he wanted to stay there, all night, drinking and feasting and adoring every prized and special inch of her.

He knew this girl like he knew himself. And he still wanted to know her *more*.

He knew he only had Lucky Charms for breakfast when she did, so he could eat her marshmallows. He knew she had her cereal with almond milk. He knew when she got painting fever she would disappear into her studio for months and not care whether the world kept spinning or fell apart, except for taking a moment each day to see him and Kate. He knew she'd secretly donated the first million she'd made to an orphanage and that when she was younger she'd watched *The Princess Bride* about twenty times, rewinding and replaying the part when the hero tells the princess, "As you wish," rather than, "I love you."

He knew that she wanted his praise tonight.

He had seen the uncertainty underneath the confidence in those striking blue eyes of hers, could see the eager rise and fall of her pretty breasts.

More than anything, he wanted to shower her with the praise she wanted. He wanted to take off that slinky black dress with his teeth so she knew how badly he craved her. Then he wanted to take his teeth from her tiny toes and drag them up her shapely ankles, her firm calves, her slim beautiful thighs, and roam his hands up her tiny waist and her beautiful breasts while he buried his lips between her legs and drowned in the intoxicating taste of her. He wanted to take her to heaven, because that was the place where angels live, and he wanted her to ask something of him—anything—so that he could look into her eyes and tell her, "As you wish."

But he did none of that.

Could not do it. Not yet.

Because she'd worn this dress tonight for another man. And the thought of that alone made him feel like kicking a kitten.

"I can feel your eyes on my back, Jules." Molly broke into his thoughts, probably sensing his overwhelming testosterone encircling her.

He leaned on the door frame with his wide shoulders, still struggling to process this new feeling of complete and utter jealousy. "You're showing off so much skin I'm concerned you're contracting pneumonia as you stand there," he said.

She swung around in surprise. Her mouth hung open, and then she tossed her head back and laughed. "Really?

You're concerned about my health? Or about your ego and the fact that you can't even admit to me for one night in my life that I don't look like I came out of a fistfight and a blender?"

His fingers curled into his palms and his lips clamped shut. So…she thought he'd insulted her?

"If you don't want to be mauled the entire evening, I suggest you at least find a sweater," he instructed. He was trying to sound friendly. Like a good friend. A best friend would make such a suggestion, wouldn't he?

"It's a hundred degrees outside. Why would I need a sweater?"

He stared down pointedly at her breasts—yes, so that she noticed—then back up at her until she squirmed under his stare. "Need I remind you you're my lover for the time being? You're like a property of mine and I won't have any of those bastards…staring at your…your *assets*."

"I'm like five feet tall and almost invisible, Jules. Nobody's going to stare except, hopefully, Garrett. And then he'll propose and we'll have babies together."

Over my dead, rotting body, you will!

He was a hair from hyperventilating by now. "I didn't sign up to play the part of the freaking fool, Molls. What am I supposed to do while you hold court at the family gathering? You're supposed to be *my* girl!"

Her eyes sparkled in mirth, because she'd probably never seen him worked up to a lather before. "Well, at least you can give your big 'guns' a good workout as you fend off my unwanted suitors, huh."

He stalked over and grabbed her shoulders, not amused and very freaking jealous about all this. "Damned right I will, and you know why?"

"Enlighten me."

"All the guys in attendance, from Landon's friends to

business associates, are going to swarm you like a pack of starving beasts. They always have, and you don't even notice. You're so damned different, Molly..." She had no idea, no idea what she did to him or anyone else. She was not only blind to him, she was blind to all men. The looks she received while she was staring off into space, thinking of a painting, were never even noticed.

Had she forgotten all the invitations she'd had to prom? She hadn't even attended, but she goddamned well had been asked.

"You really think I'm different, Jules? You know, maybe that's because of my special relationship with my Oster!"

He laughed and wondered when the hell he would hear the last of that. *Never,* he thought, then growled in frustration and clenched her shoulders. "You don't need to change one whit about you to catch a man. If you need to change your identity to make him see something great about you, then Garrett doesn't deserve you. None of those bastards do."

Something he said struck a chord. Molly stopped fiddling with the bag and clutched it firmly to her abdomen. She surveyed him in curious speculation and tilted her head a notch, those sky-blue eyes wide with innocent expectation.

"So basically," she said, her lips lifting at the corners, those same lips he wanted to kiss more than anything until they were red and swollen and only his. "So what you're saying is—I *do* look good?"

Julian stood ramrod stiff as he struggled to reply, not wanting her to be seen like this by anyone. Anyone. But he owed her the truth and he had to shove his jealousy aside if it killed him.

And it was. Killing him.

Looking at her like this. Killing him.

Wanting her and having to wait. *Killing him.*

He twirled his finger in the air and thickly commanded, "Give a little spin for me."

She spun, slowly. Yep, killing him. Her butt was so perky and round he could already feel it in his hands. Needing to do something—touch her, anywhere—he reached out to tuck a loose tendril of red hair behind her ear, then his lips curled ever so slightly on one side as he inclined his head just a fraction, and said in a gruff voice, "Yeah, baby. You look good." And he gave that rump a little playful pat because he'd been aching to. "Too damned good."

Five

"*So do you think Garrett will like my dress, too?*"

Molly's question irritated Julian like a painful snakebite as they drove to Landon and Beth's gated home. He hesitated before at last answering her with a tender squeeze of her hands, which she'd been nervously wringing on her lap. "No doubt about it, Mopey. Just relax, you look stunning."

But now it was he, Julian John Gage, who needed to relax.

He felt like drinking hard, but he wasn't stupid enough to get drunk like the night of the masquerade party, when he'd lost control and acted like some sixteen-year-old dweeb with his first girlfriend.

Oh, no. Tonight he needed all five senses and then some.

Tonight Molly needed him to put on a show and damned if he wasn't aching to give it to her.

To *all* of his family.

But he felt like he had a bomb strapped to his rib cage

and he wondered if he'd be able to keep his usual cool. His success might depend on it. Keeping cool, biding his time, being patient. Logically, that was what he must do. But Molly was in love with his brother, dammit, and both his head and his cool had left him a week ago when he'd learned of it.

Things he had planned to do his whole life were happening, and precipitously. Regrettably, not in the manner he had intended them to.

Never had he imagined he would experience this much jealousy over the girl he'd always planned to have for himself falling in love with his brother.

God, he still couldn't believe this was true.

Still, he was trying very hard to screw his head back on and focus on enjoying the parts of the evening he knew would bring him pleasure.

Like showing off his new "girlfriend" to his family. "Mother, have you met Molly?" he could ask while the unspoken words that floated between them would be, *The woman you warned me never to touch? I'm tumbling her all night now, and she loves it. We both do. Hey, will you excuse us for a moment? We're going to go ahead and have sex out by the bushes....*

But sadly, not even that thought brought him comfort as he handed his keys over to the valet and strode over to help Molly out of the car.

Her scent dizzied him as she stood up from the low seat.

Creamy legs...silken red hair...the sexy-as-hell curve of her neck just begging to be bitten...

He wasn't going to think about that now. In silence, he focused on how warm and calm the night breeze was as he led her up the staircase, her hand unsteady in his.

"Molls?"

"Mmm?"

He wanted to tell her she had never looked more beautiful to him. Instead, he lifted her hand and placed a soft kiss on the back of it, tipping her chin encouragingly with his other hand. "We've got this," he murmured, and her instant smile wrapped around his heart.

Hand in hand, they entered the gleaming foyer of the two-story mansion, where a harpist welcomed them with a slow, haunting tune. The gathering consisted of a small group of friends and family and of course Landon's enormous mastiffs, who were plopped on the rug at the far end of the living room.

Molly had told Julian earlier that Kate and Beth's business, Catering, Canapés and Curry, was handling tonight's party.

So at least the food would be good.

As soon as Julian and Molly were spotted, they were split apart. Kate and Beth sequestered Molly for interrogation while his mother, in an evening dress and a pair of bed slippers, flew over to Julian before he could even find a server with a wine selection. "My dear son! My dear, dear son!" she called from afar, crossing the room toward him. "What's this I hear about you and Molly, JJ?"

"Mother, why did you give me two names if you did not plan to use them?" he said, exasperated.

"All right then, Julian John—answer me now and don't test me. My nerves are frazzled as it is without any help from you these days!"

A fond smile played on his lips as his mother stopped an arm's length away, regal and elegant even in slippers and panting for her breath—something only a matron like Eleanor Gage could pull off.

Julian could already taste the satisfaction of watching the "news" affect and disgruntle his overprotective mother. She, who had sent him to Spain, France, Russia and Africa to separate him from his best friend. She, who had warned him if he ever touched the only girl he'd ever truly cared for, he might as well not consider himself a part of the Gage family anymore.

Yeah, it gave him pleasure, perverse pleasure, to see if she would make good on her threats. A part of him savored the fight with her even though he loved her. It had hurt him, incredibly, to be judged and condemned by his entire family for a sin he hadn't yet committed.

He'd been punished since he was just an adolescent, and he'd been suffering ever since.

Yes. It felt good to rebel against them. To give them the exact thing they were afraid of. Because soon they would see how wrong they'd been about him. Dead. *Wrong.*

So now that she was narrow-eyed and thrusting her chin out in warning, Julian ducked his head to her height and kissed her cheek smoothly, unperturbed by her bravado. "If you heard that Molly is with me, then you heard the truth, Mother. Now you can finally make good on your threat and disown me."

Eleanor drew back with a shocked little breath, genuinely traumatized by his suggestion.

Julian wanted to assure her he didn't need the trust his father had left anymore. He could live lavishly with his savings alone, plus he already had a promising business ready to launch, with several billion-dollar companies lined up as clients for his PR services. Instead, he smiled at her to defuse the tension and tucked a wisp of ebony hair behind her ear.

"You knew this would happen, Mother," he said softly. "Just as I knew someday I'd have to prove to you how much I want her and how far I'm willing to go."

Her eyes, the only ones in the family that were green like his own, flared wide with accusation. Julian waited for her comeback, but words seemed to be failing her at the moment.

He really wished that if his mother was staring at him as if he were a monster, it was because sweet, lovely Molly was crazy about him, couldn't keep her hands off him and was letting him have his way with her in bed, in the shower, in the car, in the kitchen and in every place he could think of. And not because of this idiotic little lie.

He needed her to be his.

He didn't know how much longer he could wait, or what it would take for her to realize she and Garrett weren't compatible in any single way that she and Julian were.

"If you think I'm going to let you use that girl like all those Janes you go out with, you're sorely mistaken, Julian John. I'm like that girl's *mother*."

He nodded in agreement. He had definitely understood the position his mother had been placed in two decades ago when the Devaneys had been brought to the house. She had been a recent widow with three young sons, feeling responsible for the death of an employee who left two young daughters orphaned. His mother, always stern but nonetheless a loving woman, had taken them in, but hardened her position with her sons in the process.

It was too much on her nerves to ever think the boys would harm the girls in any way; after all, they owed them their father. And yet nobody had ever understood that Julian did not want to hurt Molly. Just as he did not want to hurt his mother now. It just was what it was.

He wanted Molly. And no one was going to stop him from having her anymore.

In feigned aloofness, he grasped one of her jeweled hands and indolently patted it between both of his. "Why don't you have a little more faith in me as well, Mother? And let us be happy together, for once." Before he left to greet Landon and his wife, he grumbled, "I'd never hurt Molly. *Ever.* And it hurts me that you even think I would."

Molly stood at the other end of the living room with Kate and Beth, who was being brought up to speed on all the excitement.

"I can't believe this. Landon and I leave for two months, we come back and you and Julian are *dating?*"

Molly waved a hand excitedly. "We're actually way past that, Beth. I've moved in already." She nodded proudly, then added, "But you know, that's exactly how shocked I felt when I emerged from a long creative streak in my studio to find out Landon had remarried. I didn't even have a clue he'd met someone. Julian should've kept me up-to-date all those nights he brought Chinese food!"

Looking past Beth, Molly spotted Landon, another gorgeous Gage specimen. He kept glancing in their direction as he addressed Julian, and although Landon was not a man easily perturbed, even *he* appeared slightly confused as he spoke to his youngest brother this evening. Garrett joined them within seconds, and Molly could just sigh at the sight of his broad back. She could imagine their next kiss and already knew it would be as hot as the first....

With a wistful smile, she watched the three men, all of whom she adored. The chandelier lights caught on Julian's streaked golden hair, which sharply contrasted with both of his older brothers' dark coloring, and she melted with tenderness for him. Just to think Julian might be taking crap from his brothers because he was supposedly dating her only endeared him to her more. Would Garrett do something like this for her?

While Julian lounged around effortlessly, seemingly careless to everything they said, Garrett stood sterner, more tense and, hopefully, already jealous. Landon, however, had never looked so utterly relaxed. Like a man completely satisfied with the state of his life and thoroughly in love, as was evident from the frequent looks he stole in Beth's direction.

"Landon said he always knew this would happen," Bethany offered in a private whisper, oblivious to her husband's attention across the room as she leaned closer to Molly. "When our plane landed, he called his office and heard about you two from Garrett. He wasn't even surprised about it. He said it was inevitable."

"He did?"

It was a shock to Molly.

Because who on earth would ever think Julian and Molly could be more than friends?

It was ridiculous. Molly didn't even like to date. And Julian was a playboy.

Plus, the Gage family still viewed her as a child, except for Garrett, who seemed to be the only one who'd realized she was now a full-grown woman. A *kissable* grown woman.

Still reeling at the idea, she looked back at the group of men, intending to admire Garrett from afar and remind herself why she was so in love with him, but her gaze snagged on Julian as he calmly explained something to his brothers.

Already having disposed of both his black jacket and his silver tie, Jules exuded powerful masculinity and self-assurance as he stood there, the cuffs of his shirt rolled up to his elbows to expose his tanned, thick forearms. His stance was so wide and confident, it seemed to say, *Yeah, baby, I own me, I own this and I own you.*

Before Molly could force her gaze back to the man she loved, Julian seemed to sense her scrutiny, for suddenly, his head turned. The smile he wore gradually vanished.

With the glittering lights overhead, his eyes, those eyes that changed from gray-green to gold-green in a moment, right now looked as green as Colombian emeralds. And they blazed at her from across the room—almost proprietarily, as if he *also* thought he owned the little black dress she wore and the pair of black panties underneath.

Molly! You did not just think of your panties!

Mortified, she jerked her gaze away, her stomach clenching, and then she had to look back at Julian. Because…surely she had hallucinated that he was giving her the Wolf vs. Red Riding Hood stare?

He said something to Garrett and started in her direction, and before Molly could understand why her insides spun in turmoil, she realized he must be putting on a show. A show so that Garrett could see that she was desirable to him. And he would get terribly jealous and feel forced to tear them apart and stake his claim on Molly once and for all.

Yes, of course. It was all part of the plan. And it was brilliant.

But as Julian walked toward her with that slow tiger prowl-walk and his stare held her captive, her legs liquefied. She hadn't felt this desirable since the night Garrett had kissed her. The way he stared at her made her feel… wanted. Womanly. So, so, womanly.

Wow, this guy was so good at this.

And he was hot.

And tonight, everyone in this room thought he was *hers*.

"Get over here and dance with me," he prodded as he reached for her with a strong, long-fingered hand.

Molly grinned. "There's no dance floor, you dope."

"Come on, Mo-Mo. There's music and that's all we need."

She smiled and took his hand, and a surprising bolt of

electricity shot through her as he clasped her fingers. He spun her into his arms and yanked her effortlessly against him, almost dizzying her with his strength.

She swallowed a small curse, unprepared to feel his powerful body aligning so perfectly with hers. And suddenly Julian had erased all the distance between them. And Molly had seen him in his *briefs*. And he was so close.

His body warmth enveloped her, causing her muscles to relax while at the same time an odd hyperawareness built inside her midsection. It...disconcerted her.

"You're so good at this, it's almost annoying," she told him with a smile.

And she hardly believed *how* good he was as she wrapped her arms around his strong nape, trying not to think of how utterly helpless she would feel if Julian was to turn on the charm with her like he did with all of his flings. Not that it would ever happen, or even that it would work. Because there could only be one man for her, and he'd *better* be watching them.

"Is Garrett looking?" she whispered, desperate to get this fake-lover charade over with. It was becoming dangerous...playing house with Julian. It was too fun and too easy. "Is he looking this way, Jules?"

"I don't know, Molls. I'm looking at you."

It was the tone he used, deep and husky as a country love song, that made her insides move in a way that made her supremely uncomfortable. Or maybe the sensation was due to the fact that Garrett must be watching them dance. It had to be. For it felt as if the Earth had stopped and not only Garrett, but the entire world, was watching them dance—or at least sway to the harp tune in the middle of Landon's living room.

"I'm pretty sure he's watching," she whispered, moving closer to Julian's ear. There, she leaned against his chest and whispered, "I'm thinking we could just stroll off somewhere and return a little disheveled, you know. Or go lock ourselves in a closet for fifteen minutes and let his imagination run wild."

She could feel the coiled tension in the muscles underneath his shirt as he dropped his head to whisper back into her ear, his lips grazing the lobe. "As you wish."

Fireflies exploded in her stomach, the words were so unexpected, as unexpected as the caressing bump of his lips against her earlobe. Molly drew back with a start, trying to calm her racing heart, telling herself he couldn't possibly know what those words did to her. Or how deeply they spoke to her. "Really?" she whispered, shaking her reaction aside. "It's a good idea?"

He arrested her gaze with tender, heavy-lidded eyes that threatened her equilibrium. All she knew was that in her favorite movie of all time, Westley looked at Buttercup in *just* this manner.

And this was just the way Garrett had to look at her by the end of the evening.

"Yeah." Julian lightly chucked her chin, then with painstakingly slowness, smoothed his calloused thumb across her lower lip in a way that made her shiver. "I've always enjoyed a little closet fun. Let's get lost."

Molly didn't remember moving so fast in her entire life—even though she had to stop several times because she was laughing so hard—than when Julian dragged her down the long hallway. She felt intoxicated with an incredible sense of freedom and mischief and fun—and when she caught a glimpse of Julian's sexy, curvy smile, she wanted to fling herself into his arms and kiss him from the excitement alone.

Within seconds he came to an abrupt stop and efficiently shoved her inside a small downstairs office.

The instant the door closed after him, Molly's heart stopped.

Darkness enveloped them. Silence and seclusion spread between them, around them, like a cloak of velvet. But in this closed space, nearly entirely occupied by a big mahogany desk, Julian's scent suddenly stormed around her like a tornado, and it made her lungs burn. He smelled clean and of spices and within seconds Molly couldn't seem to stand still. Her mouth watered, and she swallowed.

"Do you have lipstick in your purse?" he asked in a voice roughened with exertion.

Her eyes adjusted to the shadows, and she realized with a start that Julian was undoing the top buttons of his white shirt. Molly could barely organize her thoughts at the sight of his tanned throat being exposed, then the hollow between his collarbones, then a part of his pectorals.

She licked her lips and, without even thinking, she lunged at him.

Going straight for the dirty business, she coiled her arms firmly around his neck and kissed his square jaw, pressing her body against his marble-hard one. Next she trailed her lips down the length of his throat. She'd surprised him, she supposed. For he stood utterly still, maybe not even alive.

Oh, no, but he was definitely alive, very much so. His warmth seeped through his clothes and spread heat all the way to her bone marrow. Intoxicated by the incredible feel of his taut, warm skin under her roaming lips, Molly trailed a path of kisses down to his collarbone, where she crazily wondered if she should just go ahead and trace it with her tongue.

"Molly?"

Julian's voice was a thick rasp.

"Mmm," she answered, placing a gentle kiss in that hollow at the base of his throat.

"You could've used your lipstick straight on me, baby. You didn't have to kiss me."

It took a moment for that guttural whisper to register. She had been happily—maybe too happily—dragging her lips along the thick tendons of his throat so that they ended up smeared peach and no one doubted, not even Julian and especially not Garrett, that Molly had kissed him.

She stopped abruptly and backed off in sudden confusion, all of her body heat concentrating on her cheeks. "What do you mean…? I don't even remember where I left my purse, I think Beth has it."

He must have heard the utter embarrassment in her voice, for he gathered her back against him, his voice even thicker and rougher than before. "Shh. Go on then. This works, too."

But she hesitated, her cheeks now scalding. As though encouraging her, Julian undid another button of his shirt, so leisurely that as she watched she began to focus on details she had never thought of before. How gracefully his fingers moved. How both their breaths ricocheted off the walls of the small space.

How she could feel his eyes burn like lasers through the top of her head as she watched him undo another button.

How a hot little tingle spread across every inch of her skin.

And how this would all be so easy to dismiss if she hadn't seen him almost *naked*…

"Now try kissing me a little lower."

He spread his shirt open, fully open, and Molly's windpipe clamped shut. Her knees wobbled in place. Jules could be a sculpture, he was so defined and so lean. At such a short distance, he looked even *more* ripped, like a top athlete. Molly could see every square indentation of his wash-board abs, every sharp rise and fall of muscle.

A tremor rushed through her, and when she didn't move, he slipped his hands onto the back of her head and gently urged her toward him. His fingers were long and felt gentle on her scalp, and as she set her palms on his rib cage and bent her head to his collarbone, she felt his fingertips work on her butterfly clasp and undo her hair.

A hot little shiver rushed from the top of her scalp to the tips of her toes as her hair tumbled to her shoulders. Trembling, she lowered her head and set a dry kiss on the V of his neck. Gingerly at first, holding her breath, trying to suppress another tremor building inside her body. Julian stood utterly still, and she wondered if he held his breath, too. Then she heard him softly say, "Go lower."

Her eyes drifted shut and she set down another kiss, pressing her lips lightly against the tautly stretched skin above his six-pack. She felt the muscles contract under her fingerprints, and her tummy clenched in response. Why did she feel so shaky? Why was her mind spinning inside her cranium? She felt like a teenager stealing a first kiss, like a bad girl misbehaving, which she'd never been before. Of course it was all due to the excitement of making Garrett jealous. She had to remind herself all these emotions were due to the fact that her and Julian's plan was so good, it was going to *work*.

"Lower, baby," he murmured in a thick, raspy voice.

She was so trusting of Julian that she almost automatically obeyed, following his instructions without hesitation, while in the back of her mind she started to wonder how he would get Garrett to see that Molly had kissed his washboard abs, too. Daydreaming of Garrett's jealous face while a strange liquid fire simmered through her veins, she let her lips wander lower, Julian's skin hot and silky under her lips…her heart thundering in her ears as she heard him once again rasp, "Lower." Feeling like she was dreaming, she went lower, her eyes feeling heavy as a strange tremor tingled along her nerve endings, until she heard him unzip his pants.

Startled, she lifted her head in confusion. He was laughing down at her, his eyes sparkling in the shadows, those sensual lips curled at the corners as he zipped back up.

"You're so innocent, Molls. I was wondering when you'd catch on," he said.

She smacked his elbow and straightened, already feeling a rush of color climb up her cheekbones. "You jerk!"

She tried pushing him aside but he seized her wrists and yanked her back to him, his laughter lingering in his voice. "No, no, no, not yet, baby. We need to work on you now."

He rumpled her hair with those long-fingered hands and Molly felt herself clam up, her throat closing with an unnameable emotion. She felt…unsteady. Vulnerable and open to him. Even those feathery touches on her scalp felt special. Electric. Rushing from the roots of her hair to her brain, charging her with inexplicable adrenaline.

As he worked on her hair, the mist of his breath fanned, warm and minty, across her forehead, and she had to use all her effort to fight the impossible flames flicking through her body. His smell was killing her. Dizzying her.

What was happening to her?

This was Julian, not Garrett. *Julian*.

She sucked in an unsteady breath, and his hands went still on the crown of her head. Their eyes locked in the dark as his hands slid down to her nape as he slowly ducked toward her. Closer. Closer.

She was frozen in place, her voice a breathless whisper. "Julian…what are you doing…?"

"Shh. I just want some of your lipstick on my mouth.

Just a little." His breathing changed as he secured her cheeks between his big hands, and she became aware of the bite of something incredibly large and rigid against her stomach.

"Julian…" she said, turning her head to the side. Their noses brushed accidentally, but rather than pull back, Julian dipped his head even farther and scraped his mouth purposely across hers.

The contact singed.

Her mouth parted on a gasp.

Julian pulled back, his eyes gleaming in the darkness. Then he lowered his head and repeated the motion, scraping his mouth across hers. Her legs went rubbery, her core melting like lava.

A little quiver rippled through her, followed by a surge of desire so sharp and powerful, her world tilted on its axis. Not even Garrett's kiss had done this to her. Nothing on this earth had *ever* done this to her. She shouldn't feel such blazing need swimming through her veins, shouldn't want to feel more, feel everything.

But she did, goodness, she did.

His nearness intoxicated her, the brush of his sensual lips fascinated her beyond measure, and she felt weak with wanting, had never wanted anything so much as she wanted to be kissed by him. Right now, in this tiny lightless room, this very instant. Kissed thoroughly and deeply by this sex god everyone wanted but no one could ever have. Least of all Molly.

But Julian did not kiss her. Only teased her with the possibility of it. The delicious scent of his body enveloped and dizzied her. It was incredible; this feeling of flying. He was so familiar and at the same time totally new. As if discovering your body could do something you never expected it to. This was how it felt to awaken to Julian John. And that was the only word she could think of. *Awaken.*

To Julian John.

He just had to kiss her.

Please kiss me

Her breathing escalated and her lips parted as he scraped his mouth across hers for the third time. She heard a sound come out of herself and almost collapsed in a puddle on the floor when he released her.

"There. I'm probably wearing more lipstick than you are now. Come on, Mo-Mo. Let's get out of here."

He went to open the office door, and light from the corridor spilled in, silhouetting his magnificent form. Their eyes met across the gloom while he waited for her to get her bearings. But her knees felt like soup.

Her legs like noodles.

She blinked but couldn't focus.

She couldn't even breathe.

She didn't know what was wrong with her, but her mind was screaming for him to come back, for him to kiss her, for her to kiss him, for her to do anything to be kissed by Julian John. And suddenly when he swung around to leave, she blurted out, "JJ, wait!"

Her heart stopped when he froze, and for a wild instant, all that was audible in the dark room was both their uneven breathing. Their eyes met again—and something electrifying pulsed between them.

He closed the door so slowly her heart almost disintegrated, and then she heard a click as it hit the doorjamb. Darkness swallowed them again, darkness and something wild and untamable. An unbearable intensity charged the air as he took a step forward.

Molly was not thinking right, felt drunk with sensations. With expectation. *Anticipation.*

"What did you just say?" Julian asked. His voice was very, very soft. Dangerously soft.

Molly held her breath, her lungs near bursting. "I said *JJ.*"

His eyes shimmered like lanterns in the night, and her heart rattled in her chest and the blood roared in her ears as he took that last step closer.

With slow, deliberate precision, he placed his hands on either side of her head against the back wall and caged her between his arms as he leaned forward. A gravelly sound stole into his voice as he slid his fingers through her loose hair and encircled the back of her head. "Say it to my face, Molly. Say it one more time to my face. I dare you."

Longing burst open inside her. Hunger. Want. *Everything.*

She knew this was crazy and wrong and yet she couldn't help herself, couldn't stop. Her body was trembling, head-to-toe, trembling. He had been playing a game with her and perhaps she wanted to play back, but this was more than a game.

Maybe?

Was it?

She didn't know anything anymore, except that maybe she should apologize for calling him by his most loathed nickname and just leave.

Maybe she didn't really want to be kissed by Julian John, because she wanted Garrett. Or maybe she'd truly lost her head tonight, because as she met his gaze in the shadows, she heard herself speak between panting breaths.

"I said *JJ,* JJ."

The silence was deafening.

Julian's eyes widened, for he was sure that he hadn't

heard right the first time. But this second time, he just couldn't believe it.

Molly had called him JJ, and he was going to have to make her pay for that. Stat.

In a whiplash move, he yanked her up against him and hoarsely demanded, in a voice as jagged as torn paper, "Do you remember what I told you I would do if you ever, ever called me JJ again?"

Smiling a smile that was all mischief, Molly tilted her back, her breasts rising and falling fast. She nodded slowly, provocatively—tauntingly.

The little she-cat wanted this!

Almost drugged with the thought of exacting his punishment, Julian caressed his hands up her slender arms, savoring the feel of her smooth skin against his calloused palms. "Well, then, I'm going to have to kiss you now," he purred, the words acting like foreplay as he leaned closer. He could almost taste the gloss on her lips already.

"O-okay, Jules," she said, almost a squeak as she gripped the rolled-up sleeves at his elbows as though hanging on to him for dear life.

Swamped with every single emotion in the world and close to exploding with wanting her, he cupped her face between his large hands and lowered his head, his heart going a powerful *baboom baboom baboom*. "'Okay, Jules'? Is that all you have to say? All right, then, you asked for it, Moo…now you're getting it good…"

He started easy, her face framed in his grasp as he lightly set his lips on hers, but with that whisper touch alone, lightning streaked across his veins and seared their mouths like fire. Suddenly, that single, wholly erotic fusion of their bodies lit his entire being on fire. He grabbed her closer, and she slid her hands up his bulging arms, their mouths parting hungrily in unison.

Groaning as her plush lips opened for him, he plowed his tongue into her mouth in a thirsty search for hers. Her soft moan tumbled down his throat as she shyly licked him back.

She tasted like peaches. And he *loved* peaches.

Deepening their kiss, he trailed his open palms down to the small of her back and conformed her curvy body to his. Her breasts softly pressed against his diaphragm, and it drove him crazy when she rubbed the tips of her nipples up against the wall of his chest.

Her nails bit into his shoulders while her mouth eagerly explored his, and when her hips began rocking against his, too, his senses swam with both pain and euphoria. The pain came from his pulsing length pressing against his pants zipper, aching to grind against those luscious hips she taunted him with.

His fingertips dug into her waist as he crushed her tighter to him, and plunged deeper into her mouth, stealing dozens of incredibly sweet and wet tastes of her. Ten. Eleven. Twelve. She tasted pure. And he desperately wanted to make love to her.

Undone by her wildness, he grappled with her hands and lifted them above her head, pinning her against the back wall. This surprised her, and she gasped. He caught the sound and kissed her harder. Wetter. Longer.

His body exploded in chaos as she responded in kind, pulling her arms free and rubbing her hands up his biceps, through his hair, making soft purring sounds against his mouth.

She felt incredible. *Incredible.*

He had never wanted anything or anyone more in his life. Molly. His tiny, sweet little gypsy. He wanted to hear her come undone for him, to lose control like she made him lose his.

But did she really want this? Did she have any idea how serious he was about this, about *her?*

"Molly," he murmured tenderly, then he dived down her neck and twirled a wet path to her delicate collarbone.

"Don't stop yet," she mewed in a little helpless plea, her fingertips sliding back into his hair. "Please let me pretend for a little bit."

His insides twisted with foreboding. "Don't you *dare*—" he came back up and shoved his tongue into her mouth, taking all of her taste, taking all that she could give "—pretend that I'm my brother."

But that tormenting thought now held him back like an iron chain, and he had to rest his forehead against hers with a groan, his breaths jerking in and out as he fought to get a grip. Suddenly, the reminder that Molly was making out with him to make his brother jealous gnawed a hole the size of Texas into his gut.

But her slim arms still clung to him. Her face was still tilted up to his in offering. And he could hardly think straight while she looked up at him as if she adored him.

"You look thoroughly kissed, Molly," he rasped. He cradled her beautiful face with his big hands, drinking up the dewy desire that softened her features.

She licked her lips, her pupils dilating as her gaze darted from his eyes to his mouth, up and down, up and down. He could barely speak, his voice roughened with painful, dizzying arousal.

"Should we just go out there so my brother gets to see what I've been doing to you? He'll probably think I've had my hands all over you this evening."

She made a little choking sound and dropped her face. "Jules, stop. Please don't tease."

Julian's thighs trembled as he fought for control, fought

to keep from doing more, doing everything to her. With her. "I'd just like to know if this kiss was just for Garrett—or because you want me, Molly?"

She kept her head bent, intoxicating him with the smell of raspberry shampoo that wafted to his nostrils. "Everybody wants you, Julian. Everybody. I just can't believe this. What did we do? This was so insane, so stupid!"

"Shh." He pinned her against him when she squirmed, his hands firmly curled around her shoulders as he kissed the top of her head and tried to ease her. "If you can't do this sort of stupid thing with your best friend, then I don't know who the hell you can do it with."

She shook her head but nonetheless buried her nose in the crook of his neck. "I didn't mean for this to happen. All this is your fault! For being such an expert seducer—please don't let go yet. I just want you to hold me. Jules, you smell so good…."

One two three four five six seven eight nine ten eleven twelve…

Not enough. He could count to a million and it was not. Enough. Not enough of her. Not enough time. To hold her. Be with her. Drown in her.

A groan of pent-up desire rumbled up from deep within his throat as his fingers clenched around her waist. "I wasn't seducing you, Molly—but you shouldn't have tempted me to kiss you." Unable to stop himself, he recklessly slid his hands upward to engulf her breasts as he heatedly nibbled on her earlobe. "Now I want to kiss you until you're weak and pliant in my arms. Until you tell me what it is that you really want, because I don't think you even know what you're asking for—"

"So! Are you two finished in here—or do we have to call the fire department?"

* * *

The baritone voice that cut through Julian's delicious, seductive words yanked Molly to full wakefulness. She jerked in Julian's arms as if she'd just been dumped into the frigid waters off Alaska and straightened to see Garrett— the man she wanted to marry—standing just outside the open door. Landon stood next to him, and while Landon's expression verged on amusement, Garrett did not look pleased.

And now he'll think I'm a whore.

The sudden thought popped into her mind and she almost wanted to groan in self-pity.

Her cheeks glowed hot as Julian pushed her behind him in a stance that reeked of protectiveness, and she was grateful for that. Taking advantage, she hid against his back and frantically struggled to rearrange her dress and hair.

"We'll be done as soon as you two dopes leave us alone."

How Julian could sound so calm and collected, she didn't know, because panic had gripped Molly by the throat and she could hardly even breathe now.

She'd wanted Garrett to imagine she and Julian had shared a little romp this evening. But she had never, ever expected to be caught while doing it.

What had she been thinking? She had clearly been undone by the strange, tantalizing complexity of Julian's male scent, the desperate desires his mouth evoked, his kisses always somehow bringing the heartbreaking reminder of her night with Garrett at the masquerade. Every time she kissed Julian, her chest began to *ache,* and not in a good way.

"We apologize, but Mother sent us," she heard Landon explain to Jules almost apologetically. "Not a task I was looking forward to."

"I'm surprised she didn't summon the whole party to

come stop us," Julian grumbled, and with one of his powerful arms, he slammed the door back shut.

Cursing low in his throat once they were alone, he extended an arm to keep the door closed and glanced past his shoulder.

"You okay?"

"Yes," she said as she arranged herself frantically, wanting the small room to develop an appetite and suddenly swallow her whole. She couldn't believe Julian had touched her *breasts* just now.

"The point was to look disheveled, Molls. And you do."

He sounded calm, almost too calm. When he reached into his pants pocket and handed over her butterfly clasp, Molly reached for it and clipped her hair back as best she could, her hands still trembling when she finished.

She sighed dejectedly.

What Julian had said made sense, of course. But she felt incredibly guilty and maybe still a little aroused. The things he had been saying to her before they were interrupted? The things he had been saying while he was cupping her breasts?

That was major, major stuff he'd been whispering in her ear!

"You're right," she said, avoiding his gaze, his all-knowing gaze that would intuitively pick up on just how far past her comfort zone they had gone. "This is perfect, couldn't be more perfect. You're a master, Jules. Master of disaster." She gave him a quick peck on the cheek and tried to sound businesslike. "Thank you."

Ducking under his arm, she yanked the door open and swept outside. Determinedly, she walked past both the Gage men, who stood like sentinels down the hall, with their black suits and matching impassive expressions on their faces.

She shot each of them a smile, smiling with her inflamed mouth that had just been kissed like a hussy's.

She even pretended she was proud of it.

But she could feel Julian's eyes on her back, sensed he hadn't moved from the office doorway yet, and as she rounded the corner to the busy and crowded living room, all she wanted was to find a nice spot where she could collapse safely and sort out her out-of-whack emotions.

She heard footsteps and suddenly Garrett loomed at her side, his fingers curling around her elbow. "I'd like to talk to you in private, Molly," he said. "Do you have time tomorrow?"

Surprised, she looked into her beloved's eyes while an avalanche of emotions buffeted her from the inside.

He seemed concerned, intense, his obsidian eyes peering into hers so fiercely, she feared he'd be able to see how aroused and guilty she was.

"Of course," she said with a shaky nod, her voice husky for all the wrong reasons. "I'll stop by your office at noon, Garrett."

"Thank you," he said softly, and placed a kiss on her forehead, his hands lingering on her cheeks for a second.

She was so numb that she couldn't even enjoy his caress that she'd fantasized about feeling again for days and nights.

She could hardly believe that she'd finally caught his attention.

In a daze, she crossed the living room toward Kate and Beth, her thoughts scattered and unfocused. She should be celebrating, she knew. Garrett wanted to talk to her in private tomorrow, and he was, at the very least, concerned. Maybe he was even hiding his jealousy with grave effort. By all appearances, her plan was succeeding. Wasn't that what she'd been dreaming of accomplishing?

But no. She couldn't enjoy her victory because she was too rattled by what she'd done.

What on earth had gotten into her, to tempt Julian the way she had? Were those the actions of a woman in love with another man?

And what if things became awkward with Julian now? What if this stupid charade affected the one relationship in her life she cherished above anything?

"What on earth happened to you?" Kate cried with one startled look at her.

Molly decided she was going to own up to it.

Whatever her sins, whatever her mistake, she was going to *own up to it* if it killed her.

"Julian and I made out in the dark. You should try it sometime, Kate. It was actually fun before those two idiots interrupted."

She glared in the direction of Garrett and Landon, then saw Julian stroll from around the corner of the hall, his hands in his pockets, his blond hair mussed. *Sexy* didn't begin to describe the man. He looked tousled. Delish. Thoroughly kissed, as he'd put it—and there was no question about it. Streaks of what looked like Molly's peach lipstick slashed all over his tan skin. Marking his thick throat, up along his jaw, across the side of his plush lips. He looked so rumpled he could've just battled a Siberian tiger in a cage, and for some reason, knowing the tiger had been *her* caused a pool of liquid heat to rush between her thighs.

"Julian, what happened to you?" Beth asked as he approached.

Julian's green gaze tracked and zeroed in on Molly, and her swollen mouth began to burn under the intimacy of his stare. Between her legs, she burned. Her breasts, the very breasts he had cradled in his enormous hands, pricked hotly in remembrance. Quite simply, and too damn easily, he set her ablaze with his gaze, reminding her of his blatantly sexual words, almost causing her to combust.

"Molls and I had a little fun in the downstairs office. You okay, baby?"

His voice, still husky enough to resemble the timbre he'd used in the dark, did wild things to her overstimulated senses. Awareness had quickly skyrocketed to hyperawareness in that empty office, and now she was frantic to power these sensations off.

While the other women processed his words in stunned silence, Julian made a thorough assessment of Molly's face with a measured expression on his own.

Was he worried they'd gone too far, too?

Trying to offer some reassurance, Molly let her lips curl upward, loathing this awkwardness between them. But thankfully, a playful light kindled to life in his eyes. When he gave her his wolfish smile, Molly almost sagged in relief.

Visibly relaxing, too, Julian put his arms around her and dragged her to his side, and Molly knew as she snuggled against him that whatever happened, it was all going to be all right.

As long as she had Julian.

"You know I love you, don't you?" she whispered up at him once again, kissing his hard cheek. It was not the first time she'd said it, not at all. But this time, he drew back and met her gaze, his smile fading. Then he planted a long, hard kiss on her temple, his voice gruff as he told her, in her ear, so nobody else could hear, "So do I."

Six

So here we are now, Molly thought as she rode the eleva-tor up to the top floor of the *San Antonio Daily* building the next day.

At last Garrett seemed to be ready to do something about her situation with Julian. The question was: What was he going to do?

And how was Molly going to react to it?

She honestly didn't know. Whatever happened today, though, she wore her largest earrings and her thickest ban-gles and her sassiest attitude to the meeting. It was a trick she used when she needed the extra security boost. There was just something about big jewelry that made her feel better no matter how dreary things looked or how anxious she felt. So now it was one minute until noon, and she was every bit the confident lady as she marched down the long hall that led to the executive offices.

"Molly!" Julian's assistant exclaimed with obvious

warmth, glancing up at her through her spectacles from behind an enormous desk. "I didn't know you were paying a visit! He went out to lunch...."

Smiling, Molly greeted the older woman with an affectionate hug. Ms. Watts had been with Jules forever and sometimes conspired with Molly to pull Julian out of important meetings. Just for fun.

"I'm actually here for Garrett today, Ms. Watts." But her stomach felt queasy, and suddenly she very much wished she was having lunch with Julian instead.

She was led directly into his office by Garrett's assistant, a younger woman who sat at an identically enormous desk not too far away. Molly couldn't help but straighten her spine when she was announced. "Miss Devaney to see you, Mr. Gage," the assistant intoned, and then quickly shut the doors behind her.

Over six feet tall, with dark hair and broad shoulders, Garrett stood by the window with his hands in his jacket pockets, radiating intimidation. Her knees felt knobby as she walked forward, somehow expecting to catch a glimpse of something telling in his expression. But his face revealed nothing at all when he turned around and gave her a brief, almost businesslike smile.

"Molly, I don't think I need to tell you why you're here? Or why Kate—" he signaled to her sister, whom Molly just now noticed sitting behind Garrett's desk, pretty as you please "—and I want to talk to you today."

Molly sat down across the desk from Kate, still absorbing the fact that he had not meant to have a "private" conversation with her at all. Private had merely meant without Julian present.

The realization made her scowl at him, her blackest, angriest scowl.

She couldn't help noticing Garrett seemed so detached

today, unlike the passionate lover of that magical evening. Of course, the man had excellent control, so you never knew with him. That night, he'd sure as hell surprised her, too. Now Molly looked into his eyes but try as she might, she detected no special heat as he looked at her.

Had she completely misread him? Had he been so drunk that just…any "wench" would have done? How could he stand there, so lamplike, after he'd caught her in a dark room with Julian? Even Julian, who was known to be the cool and aloof brother, looked at her with much more… Actually, Julian's looks set her on fire. But enough of that.

They were just different, the two men—and she had to stop comparing them.

She had to get it through her thick skull, once and for all, that those kisses with Julian last night had been pure error. She'd gotten carried away and she wasn't even certain why she'd done something so reckless as to tempt a lion like Julian. Except maybe she knew that he would never take things too far with her.

Or *would he?*

Because last night in bed, she'd been so tormented and confused. The things he'd whispered, the things he'd made her feel as he'd kissed her had been the most intense she'd ever felt in her life, even more than on the night—

No. It couldn't be.

How could anything top what she'd felt that night at the masquerade? Was it right to feel all this excitement and passion when just *any* guy kissed her? No. She knew it was impossible, it was too overpowering, too special.

So then what was the matter with her?

"Can you please explain to us what's going on between you and Julian?" Garrett queried, breaking into her reflections.

Completely disbelieving his tone, Molly leaned back

in her chair and crossed her arms, her bangles making a clanking noise.

Wow.

She'd really made up that whole masquerade soul-mate kiss, hadn't she?

Garrett didn't seem jealous *at all,* and now her silly thoughts of marrying him were quickly being dashed. She'd thought she was luring him in with her plan and now she wondered if he was even hungry for the hook she'd tossed him. Apparently, Garrett only had a weakness for Molly in a *wench* costume and while he was inebriated out of his ever-loving mind.

Wow. Really. She was such a dope.

"Are you two seriously going to pretend you don't know? Or do I need to spell it out to you?" Molly asked him, getting supremely irritated by all this. Where was the man who'd kissed her at the masquerade? Where was the hunger that awakened hers? The passion that had ignited hers? Had it all been a joke? A dream? A ruse?

When neither Kate nor Garrett answered and her masquerade man refused to make an appearance, her irritation increased tenfold. So they were going to drill her and intimidate her. Did they interrogate Julian like this, too?

"We're together, Garrett," Molly suddenly said, thrusting her chin out defiantly and sounding damned proud. "I moved in with him. I'm his gi—lover. And I've never been so happy." The last was true. She'd always had the most fun with Jules, had loved him beyond loving anyone else, protected him beyond anyone else. They covered for each other, laughed with each other, fought with each other....

This morning they'd had breakfast together, and they'd laughed. Even after the debacle of last night. They'd laughed.

"Did you know," Garrett said softly, his eyes kind, "this

is exactly what we feared would happen all these years. My mother, Kate, Landon and I. We feared Julian and you would dive headfirst into each other and one of you, especially you, Molly, might not make it out."

With a painful frown, Molly wondered why Garrett didn't just drop the mask already and step into his sexy black masquerade boots. He'd had *guts* that night, taking what he wanted, which had clearly been *her*. Today? He merely seemed concerned, like a brother would be, and that had definitely not been Molly's plan from the start. "Why would you think that about me and Julian?" she challenged, wanting to scoff at the accusation.

His dark eyes widened in surprise, as though Molly were lacking in brainpower to have overlooked something so obvious. Kate stepped in to explain, "Because when you were teens you were infatuated with each other, Molls. You cried when I told you he was like your brother. You cried for days and when I demanded to know why, you told me it was because of what I'd said. Because you wouldn't be able to marry him now."

Molly groaned and rolled her eyes. "I must have been ten, Kate."

"You never cry, Molly. Never. The only times I've seen you cry in your life have been all about Jules."

"Because they sent him away and it sucked!"

"There you go," Garrett said.

She scowled. "I just don't see how our relationship concerns any of you. We've had a bond since the beginning."

In fact, Molly knew the story by heart, for it had been related to her not only by Eleanor Gage, his mother, but later by Landon, Kate, Garrett, even Julian himself.

On the day the Devaney sisters had come to live at the Gage mansion, Molly had been a mere three years old.

She'd been introduced, along with Kate, to all the family members and staff, but she'd hardly paid any attention because she had a lollipop stuck in her mouth and she was gladly sucking it. Embarrassed by this, Kate had tried to convince her to hand over the lollipop, since she'd been the one who'd given it to her in the first place, but it was all to no avail. And yet while they proceeded to do the introductions, Molly's attention had fixated on the blond, green-eyed boy who looked at her in amusement. She toddled over to him, took her lollipop out of her mouth, and graciously offered it to him with a cheeky grin.

Julian had been six at the time, and even when his mother had beamed a silent command at him to refuse the germ-filled offering, Julian had shoved it into his mouth and smiled down at Molly. Just like that, they'd been instant friends.

Now Molly looked pointedly at Garrett and cocked a brow, wondering if he even remembered that story. They'd only told it about twenty times or so, if she recalled correctly. The family laughed about it, joking that what the other brothers accomplished with force, the younger brother accomplished with a grin.

"Molly." Kate clasped her hands before her in a silent plea. "I just need you to assure me that you know what you're doing. Julian's relationships don't last. In fact, he's never even had one, only one-night stands and weekend flings. You're in way over your head here, Moo!"

"I'm not his weekend fling, Kate," she defended, suddenly fierce, determined to show them she was at no risk and meant more to Julian than that, even though what she was defending was a fake liaison intended to make Garrett jealous. "What makes you think Jules would ever hurt me? He's the only guy I know that would give me a kidney if I needed one! In fact, he's so good to me I'll bet he'd even give me two!"

The worry creases on Kate's forehead only seemed to double. "You've really fallen for him, haven't you?"

It killed Molly not to be able to tell her sister the truth, so she could at least wipe that worry off her pretty face, but then how could she assure her what a lie her relationship with Julian was, when she herself couldn't understand why she'd even kissed him yesterday?

Since she'd moved in with him, she'd been bombarded with strange feelings and emotions, hardly getting any sleep as she lay in her bed, wondering about all the *what-if*s and *could be*s in her life.

Saying good morning to him in his sexy pajamas with his six-pack abs showing was torture. Bantering with him, wanting to be close to him...

She didn't even know what she felt anymore.

She'd wanted to find love in her life, because she'd already found success in her profession. Wasn't it normal to always want something? But this time she sensed that what she wanted was nearby, but she couldn't put a name to it, and that frustrated her out of her mind.

She'd been counting on Garrett to reignite the spark in her today, not leave her feeling cold and empty. She'd been counting on this meeting where he could help her straighten out her head, and more importantly, her emotions.

Instead, she and Julian were being attacked, and it made her want to stick her claws out for him. For them. For what they had, which nobody had ever really understood in the first place.

"Julian would never hurt me," she said as she rose, fighting to keep from shouting. "I promise you if you ever see me cry because of him, I give you permission to shoot me."

"I'd actually prefer to shoot *him*," Garrett said drily.

Whipping around to face him, Molly stared at this large,

handsome man, thinking he'd always been a great influence in her life. He'd always felt responsible for her father's death. Even though the Devaney sisters had never blamed him for what had happened, it seemed as if Garrett would never forgive himself.

Which sometimes made his smiles seem sad. And made him try too hard to make things right for Kate and Molly, protect them. But…protect Molly from Julian? *Oh, puleeze!* Julian had been as crucial as sunshine to her since she was a toddler. He'd been her hero before she even heard of the word or understood its meaning.

Garrett was a good man, a great man, in fact, and Molly knew he would be a faithful and giving husband if he could only give himself a chance. But did he need to be drunk to let go the way he had at the masquerade?

Whatever the reason, she feared that the man who'd kissed her that night was an illusion. And if she'd ever, ever doubted whether she would have to choose between Garrett and Julian, it was an easy choice now that she was faced with it.

Her hero won outright.

"What is your problem with Julian anyway?" Molly asked, aghast and affronted. "Both of you—you're always riding him about something. If I were him, I'd…never talk to you again."

She pivoted for the door, but Garrett's voice stopped her.

"That little toad is my brother. Of course I love him. We merely feel responsible to protect you."

She grabbed the knob and turned. "If I need protecting from anything, I will tell you, but the last person on this earth I need protecting from is Julian." She yanked the door open and then added, "And if you love your brother so much, then I suggest you try to make things work around here before he leaves the *Daily* for good—Lord knows *I* would! Who the hell can even work in peace with this sort of constant criticism? I'm glad he's ready to move on!"

"Excuse me?"

"You heard me!" she shot back.

She gave Kate a look that said *don't do this to me again,* and with that, she stormed outside.

"Molly!" Garrett followed her, stopping her a couple of feet from where his secretary was busily tapping her computer keypad. "Where's my brother going? Is he leaving the *Daily?*"

"I want to go now, Garrett," she grumbled, trying to pull her arm free.

He drew her closer. "He's leaving the *Daily,* isn't he?"

Hating herself for having spoken so rashly, Molly dropped her face. "I think you misunderstood," she hedged.

"No, I didn't. I know he's not happy here, Molly. I've been suspecting for a time now. But if you aren't telling me when he's leaving or where, then at least answer me this. Do you love him?" he asked.

Molly stared up at the man she'd once thought she loved and wondered why her throat closed up in a tight little ball. Why she wanted to wail her heart out to him over that question alone.

Because of course the answer was yes, a thousand times *yes*.

She loved Julian in so many ways, she hadn't even begun to discover them all. And she feared that loving him as a friend was only one of them.

Halting just a few feet from his own office door, Julian saw them. Molly and the "love of her life," together at last.

He saw them say goodbye. Saw his brother pat her back. Saw her take a little sob and drop her face into his jacket. Saw him put his arm around her.

His blood simmered. His heart caved in on itself. And suddenly red-hot anger coursed through his veins and his eyes blurred with the force of his fury. Maybe this was what Molly had wanted all along. She had practiced with Julian last night so she could get out here and make Garrett jealous, make him see her as the lovely, sexy, grown woman that she was.

Perhaps Julian should've stepped back and let his best friend be coddled by the man she wanted to be coddled by.

He should laugh it off, not care. But it mattered very much. *Too* much.

Body shaking, he was amazed he could speak so calmly, so softly, as he walked up to them. "I hate to break up your tête-à-tête, but if you don't take your hands off Molly, I'm going to beat your face until our own mother won't recognize you."

Garrett stiffened, but his arms instantly dropped as his head whipped toward his. "What the hell is wrong with you, Jules?"

Julian gritted his teeth as Molly swung around in surprise. Ignoring Garrett, he stretched out his hand to her, palm up, and gazed intently into her red-rimmed eyes. She'd been crying, or about to cry. Dammit, why? He pursed his lips in anger. At her, at himself, at this entire mess he'd gotten himself into.

He'd wanted time to let things unfold naturally.

He didn't want to pull all the stops he used with other women and seduce the hell out of her. Because this was the only girl who knew him, respected him, admired him—he was *real* with her. He wanted it to be perfectly natural with her. No bull. And it just wasn't happening that way, dammit. "What day is today, Molly?"

She sniffled, then wiped the corner of her eye with one fingertip. "Um?"

"What day is it?"

She told him the date, and he nodded gravely and bent to whisper in her ear so that nobody would hear his words but *Molly*. "Exactly. You're still my girl. Aren't you? We said a month. Didn't we?"

She blinked as he drew back to survey her reaction, and when her gaze strayed to Garrett, Julian's chest tightened with rage.

Garrett, his brother.

Whom he suddenly, profoundly abhorred.

Her tear-streaked blue eyes came back to him, and she nodded and mumbled, "Of course. Take me home, all right?" And to Garrett, she said almost placatingly, "Thanks for the chat. Think about what I told you before I…stepped out, okay?"

Garrett nodded before Julian led Molly by the elbow toward his assistant's desk. He barked a dozen orders, then led Molly with him to the elevators.

Neither spoke on the drive home.

"So tell me," Julian finally said as they entered his apartment, his emotions having fermented during the drive. He was close to exploding now. "Tell me what he did to make you cry like this."

Molly stared at him with wide, shining eyes that made him want to wrap her up in his arms and keep the world from so much as looking at her, she looked so damn lost and so damn vulnerable. Her voice was a soft, puzzled whisper. "What's wrong with you today?"

He drew a deep breath, then let it all out. "He doesn't deserve you, Molly! I know a guy who's so crazy about you, he would do anything to be with you—*anything*. He'd lie for you, cheat for you, steal for you—"

She scoffed, everything sounding more ludicrous to her

by the second. "Are you getting high on my paint supply? Who are you talking about? Who would do such a thing?"

"Take a wild guess, Molls."

"I have no clue what you're talking about!"

"I could kill him for making you cry like this." Julian sat down on the living room sofa and threw his shoes off with a bang. "This obsession with my brother just pisses me the hell off, Molly. Like nothing in my life has ever pissed me off before."

She crossed her arms, suddenly glaring. He might have been pissed off, but he had no idea what was wrong with her. That she cried because she realized the entire masquerade night had been a stupid illusion in the first place. That the man she'd thought she loved…just wasn't the Garrett she knew. And like all the other men she'd ever met in her life, he would end up paling to Julian in every possible way she could imagine.

But how could she admit to this man, whose respect she craved and wanted above all others, that she just might have screwed it all up and was not really in love with Garrett? That the man she wanted was…unattainable. And that his brother and her sister had been warning her away from him because he would hurt her?

Oh, how she'd wanted to tear their eyes out when she heard them! Even if they might be right.

She gnawed on her lower lip and said nothing, focusing instead on getting ready to vent her frustrations on the only person she could vent with.

Julian.

"Just tell me what you see in him all of a sudden that you find so irresistible. Tell me why you'd go cry on his shoulder and not with *me*."

Oh, God, what was happening to her?

Her legs went flaccid with a mere look into those stormy

green eyes. He was so handsome, his jaw square and rigid, his eyebrows two sharp, bleak slashes. He was more enraged than she'd ever seen him before. She could even think he was *jealous,* and the thought summoned a deep, dark stirring in her that she'd been feeling more and more frequently lately—at the most inconvenient times. A powerful little ache in her body that craved for him to wrap his arms around her and... She didn't know what she wanted him to do.

She ached for closeness with him, almost trembled with the need. She wanted to smell his scent all around her and to feel his hands everywhere and enjoy the hardness of those big, big biceps bulge as he held her imprisoned against his body. She wanted him so close, closer, closest. As if mere friendship was no longer enough with him. As if revealing every intimate detail of her life to him, her fears, her desires...

Was. Not. Enough.

Anymore.

"Are you planning to answer me, Molly?"

Molly's throat seemed to be working extra hard to get the words out. She didn't know why her nipples were beaded under her cotton turquoise sundress, why the way Jules was shooting fire at her with his eyes made her breathless and shaky and strange. She fought against the sensations, struggling to focus on his question.

She threw her hands up in the air in frustration. "I don't know, Jules! All right? Maybe I hated when he was overly protective of us, the way he took it upon himself to chaperone you and me. He never let us have fun together, like we were doing something wrong, and we *weren't*. You may be hot for anything that walks but he never realized that we were always just friends. But I truly don't think he was being deliberately mean. Maybe he was just trying to do the noble thing out of caring and respect for me and out of respect for my father, who protected him." She softened her voice as she tried to save the last remains of her hope.

Julian's glare could have melted all the ice in Alaska. "Garrett pulled you away from me because he knew that— He knew I—" His face darkened, and Molly's nipples pricked with wanting as she watched his fingers curl into fists at his sides. An image of those fingers clutching her breasts when he'd whispered sexy confessions into her ear returned to her, and she swallowed. This was *so* not the time to get worked up about that.

Jumping to his feet, he plunged a frustrated hand through his hair and thoroughly ruffled it. "And what about him and Kate? Hell, Molls, have you not seen the way your sister looks at him? You're both pining away for the same man."

Molly blinked in stupefaction, her eyebrows pulling low when she registered what he'd said. "You're lying. You—you can't mean that— Kate doesn't feel that way about him."

"Kate is like a sister to me. I know lust when I see it, Molls."

Horrified, Molly gaped at the thought of her sister loving Garrett. So quietly? And for how long? It couldn't be.

Fiddling with one enormous hoop earring, she shook her head several times. "Jules—you don't understand. Garrett and I have *done* things. We kissed one night and it was… magical, like it was meant to be."

Freezing in place as though she'd said something monumental, Julian openly gawked at her until his expression emptied into such a blank look that it might have been comical if she didn't find it thoroughly alarming. "He *kissed* you?"

Molly offered him an embarrassed little nod, then

groaned in self-pity and buried her face in her hands. "I've never felt such a connection in my life except with you. What I felt that night seemed so real, it was like we recognized each other, like we knew we were soul mates…"

But it was all an illusion, and I can't understand it and I'm so confused.

Julian stalked a short distance away as though he didn't know what do with himself, and then he returned, his jaw muscles working restlessly. "You're kidding me, Molly. Say it now, Molls. Right. Now. Tell me you're kidding me, Moo."

She could only imagine how it looked to him, the guy she had been devouring with her lips yesterday, that she'd let his brother do that, too. What was wrong with her? Why had she felt nothing when she'd looked at Garrett today?

But it *had* happened.

Hadn't it?

"I'm not even sure it was real anymore," she admitted as she fell on the couch and covered her face with her hands. "It all happened at that loathsome masquerade, when I was wearing that stupid wench costume you dared me to wear! He…he was wearing all black. I was outside and thought it was you, and then he kissed me, and we did some intimate things, and I noticed the ring he was wearing as he held me, and I knew that it must be him."

The deafening, tomblike silence that followed stretched so long and taut, she sat up in confusion and studied Julian in growing alarm.

Suddenly, he stormed down the hallway like a man possessed, and Molly sighed and rubbed her temples to ward off a headache. She just hoped he hadn't gone to fetch a gun or something, for what was she going to do now? She was usually the impulsive one and always counted on *Jules* being the one with a cool head.

She considered following him, talking some reason into him, explaining that it was just a kiss and all that, but then he returned less than a minute later and produced something shiny from his pants pocket.

He sounded livid now. Livid.

"You mean this ring, Molly?"

Seven

As Molly stared at the ring he was holding between his two fingers, a horrific sensation crawled up her stomach like a tarantula.

She blinked several times, and her jaw fell open. "Wh-what are you doing with that?"

Garrett used to wear it all day, every day. The platinum was scratched and dented with age, for it had been in the family for generations, boasting at its center a rare blue diamond that was supposed to be worth millions.

"It's my ring. *Mine*. I won it from him. Over a month ago. He bet me that it was worth more than my autographed Mark McGwire seventieth-home-run baseball when he was *really* freaking drunk. He was off by several hundred thousand and lost the bet." Julian smiled at her, a sharp, angry smile that cut through her skin like the clean, expert slice of a dagger. "I just wear the ring to piss him off sometimes when I know I'll be seeing him."

All the color drained from her face, as though all the blood in her body was going straight to her heart, which was racing in her breast like a mad thing. If her ears were hearing correctly and her dazed brain processing correctly, it seemed that he was basically admitting to owning that ring on the night of the masquerade. The night that a stranger had kissed her ever-loving heart out.

Oh. My. God.

The conclusion she'd come up with terrified her. Julian…had been the one wearing that ring? Julian had whispered…those sexy words in his raspy voice while his big, long-fingered hands had touched her so provocatively…?

Julian. Her hero. Her protector. Her best friend. Her young crush. Her lifetime love.

It had been Julian who'd kissed her and made her have an orgasm while he'd fondled her? How he must have laughed! Laughed at her naïveté, at her stupidity, at her…

"I can't believe," he breathed softly, his eyes glowing like golden moons, "that you wouldn't know that I was the one who kissed you that night."

Grief and unexpected humiliation cut through her like a thousand knives. Julian had known all this time.

Her chest constricted so tightly she thought she would break apart, but she still stubbornly shook her head from side to side. "I don't understand."

His kisses. Oh, dear, his kisses. Three total. Each one so different. One, passionate and drunk. The next, cocky and trying to show off in front of Kate. And the last one, in a dark room, where it was just him and her, supposedly playing a game….

Please no, I can't be that stupid.

"I don't understand," she repeated, more frantic now.

In three steps, he closed the distance between them, and

when his fingers curled around her arm, Molly could feel the leashed power in his hold, see how he visibly fought for control. "I think I do. You thought I was Garrett that night—when I kissed you hard enough to make your mouth swell under mine. You let me put my hands between your legs, touch your breasts, maul you like a—"

"Stop it, Julian. *Stop it!*"

She leaped away and backed off, hardly able to look into those fiercely jealous green eyes, which were only reminding her that he—he who was her *everything*—had done all that. Every bit of what he'd said, and more.

Julian had kissed her, had turned her life upside down with his touch. He'd made her shatter in his arms, and then he'd acted as if it had meant nothing. *Nothing.*

He was her best friend, and yet he'd kept her in the dark all this time. He'd been intimate with her, had made her feel as if he wanted her, cherished her, but instead he'd been happily helping her seduce his own *brother!*

"How *dare* you!" she exploded at that. "How dare you do that to me and then say nothing!"

His eyes flashed, and he threw his arms up in the air. "What did you want me to say? That it was a mistake? That I got carried away by your pretty blue eyes and the way you looked in that scrap of a dress?" he shot back. "You *told me* not to mention it, and since I was drunk and clearly screwed up, I thought it was a damned good idea. You pretended nothing happened the next day, and I *went* with it. At least it gave me time to get it right."

"Get *what* right, you idiot? You just shot our friendship to hell!" She pushed him aside and stormed away to her bedroom, adding as she went, "Now excuse me if I go pack, you…you jerk! How could you even agree to help me seduce Garrett after you touched me like you did, you… Oh! *I can't even think of a word for you!*"

She slammed the door with a bang.

Her lungs burning for air, she fell back weakly against the door and stared at the bed with blurry eyes. She glanced at the walk-in closet, tempted to leave this very second. She would leave. Of course she would. But she needed him to drive her, or Kate to come get her, and she'd die before she made that request of either of them right now.

A desolate sensation weighed heavy on her chest as she thought of the mural waiting upstairs, a safe haven for her to get lost in a sea of color. She had never left a work unfinished and she was not going to start now because of that…that douche!

She would finish it tonight, or at least try to, and then she'd leave tomorrow.

She still couldn't believe it. He had known…all along, all this time. The bastard had already kissed her, fondled her, known how easy it was to make her explode.

What mockery.

That beautiful masquerade kiss now mocked her. Her best friendship in the world—her entire life—mocked her.

One after another, memories flashed before her eyes, and there wasn't a single happy memory that she could remember not featuring Julian. She saw him smiling down at her like a lone wolf, tweaking her nose, rumpling her hair, driving her back home. She saw him snarling at her and teasing her and tickling her, and calling her Mo-Po, Mopey, Moo, Molls, Mo-Mo, Moo-Moo.…

Nausea rose up her throat, and she shakily sat down on the edge of the bed, held a pillow to her chest and drew in deep breaths. But she didn't seem capable of filling her lungs. She'd just never felt so empty. So stupid. So used. Nothing in her life had ever hurt this much, not even when Jules had left her all those times.

But he won't make me cry anymore, she thought angrily, remembering Kate's recent words.

Teeth gritted, she curled up into a rigid little ball with the pillow firmly grasped to her core, and something very deep inside her clenched tight as the images of that night bombarded her once more.

His mouth, firm and urgent, the roughened sound he made as he kissed the tops of her breasts, as if he'd just entered heaven and they had been made just for him.

The way he'd groaned and bent his head to her ear, biting the lobe hungrily, desperately, and then how he'd soothingly murmured to her, "Shh…shh…"

Her eyes stung with unshed tears. How could she not have known?

She'd been so sure it was him at first, that wolfish smile so familiar to her, but then the way he'd fiercely kissed her had been so completely unlike her cocky best friend. Why did it have to be him? The man couldn't keep his hands to himself and just had to have a piece of her, too?

She'd promised herself when she was a thirteen-year-old girl that she would not shed any more tears for Julian John. He meant too much to her, was too special to her, made her feel like a princess being rescued by a hero. She'd promised herself she would get rid of the infatuation she had with him, her silly crush, because everyone told her he would hurt her and they couldn't all be wrong.

But it was no use because now the truth stared her in the face, and yes, yes, yes, it mocked her, too.

The man she'd felt she'd die if she didn't kiss again…

The man she knew in her gut was her soul mate…

That man was the only man in the world who could really, truly break her heart into such tiny particles she would never be able to piece herself back together.

And now even their friendship, the one golden and steady thing in her life, was gone.

Julian wanted to punch something.

He paced his room for hours, restless, his emotions gone berserk. Jealousy coursed through his veins like some sort of acrid poison as he remembered Molly's moans, the way she'd responded to him the night of their first kiss, like her body was a harp only his fingers knew how to pluck and tune and play...

And all while she'd thought he was Garrett.

His brother.

The guy who'd been holding her when she was in tears today.

The guy who'd owned every one of her desires for weeks.

The guy whom he very much wanted to kill right now.

He replayed the scenes over and over in his mind, recalling the hurt in Molly's eyes when he'd set her little head straight this evening. When he'd told her that he was the man who had kissed her that night, touched her so intimately and made her go off like a hot, beautiful firework in his arms. Goddammit, she'd almost seemed disappointed he hadn't been Garrett!

He gritted his teeth at the thought, deeply regretting not confronting her about it the day after the masquerade. All this time she'd been hunting for his brother thinking of *Julian's kiss*. To hell with whether she wanted to talk about it or not! If he'd done things right, he might have been holding her in his arms all this time—and not under false pretenses—and kept her from noticing Garrett. All these sleepless nights. Nights she'd wanted to have a friendly sleepover with him—yeah, right. As if he could stand being in the same bed with her without turning into some ravenous, sex-starved maniac.

Did she not *see* he'd been crazy about her for twenty years?

He had thought he could screw Molly out of his head, but clearly that had not worked. Okay, so he'd kissed her when he was drunk and hadn't talked to her afterward. Not suave. She'd expected better of him? Yeah, well, that made two of them. He wasn't too pleased to find out that she'd thought all along that it was his brother who'd kissed her.

Now they both felt like fools.

Groaning in despair, he plopped down on the bed, full of rage and agony and disgust. He couldn't stand the impotence he felt. Restless, he changed into his pajama pants and yanked back his bedcovers, but all he did was toss and turn restlessly on the bed.

So maybe he should've talked to her about that evening. Except he'd thought it best to forget about one drunken night's kiss and continue with his plans until he could do things the right way.

Well, he sure as hell was mucking it up right now, wasn't he?

No way was he going to stand for it. Suave Julian, they used to call him. How he was so cool, aloof. Yeah, right. Clearly not where Molly was concerned. His Achilles' heel. But also his greatest strength. If he had become someone and done something with himself, it was all because of that incredible redhead in his life and his desperation to show his family that he was worthy of her.

Shoving the covers aside, he stalked across his bedroom and out to the hall, where moonlight streamed through the living room windows and across his apartment.

He found the door to her bedroom ajar. He rapped his

knuckles on the wood, waited a second, then pushed the door open wider.

Her bed sat empty. It hadn't been slept in.

Scowling, he stalked the entire apartment, every square foot, and found it empty.

Heart pounding seriously hard now, hard enough to crack one of his ribs, he jammed the elevator buttons and rode up to the penthouse, his mind racing with a thousand thoughts per minute, shouting out its conclusion: *she left, she left, she left, you idiot!*

But when the elevator doors opened, he saw her.

She lay on the marble floor of his new offices, dressed in nothing but a giant button-down shirt, her hair a pool of red fanning behind her as she slept with her hands tucked under her left cheek. He drank up her image as he approached her, drinking up her image, the perfect image of this woman he'd loved since they'd first met.

She should not be sleeping on the floor. God, never on the floor.

She deserved a bed, pillows, satin sheets and a man to love her with all the passion that she unfailingly conveyed in each of her artworks.

His eyes glued to her moonlit face, he knelt at her side— she was just so damned beautiful his eyes hurt. A streak of green paint crossed her forearm to her elbow, and he ached to trace it with his fingers, then with his lips. He noticed the empty paint tubes scattered around her sleeping form and glanced up at the colorful wall before him. His heart wrenched with regret when he realized she'd been trying to finish the mural.

So she could leave.

Leave him for good.

Now, when JJG Enterprises was almost ready for his final walk-through and just days away from opening to its employees. Now, when he had grown accustomed to her being here as he met with contractors, architects, painting her heart away on a wall that had been empty before she'd made it come to life with little playful flicks of her dainty hands.

She wanted to leave now, when Julian was days away from fulfilling one of his dreams and ready to focus on the next one—the possibility of sharing the rest of his life with her.

Throat dense with emotion, he stroked the curve of her cheek with the back of one fingertip.

She sighed contentedly at that, relaxed in her sleep. Shoving aside his hesitation, he reached out, gently scooped her up and carried her back to the elevator. She was as light as a feather and as warm as a little chicken, and his chest swelled when she sought out his heat and snuggled closer. But when the audible chime signaled their arrival on his apartment floor, Molly grew heavy in his arms, and he saw her spiky titian lashes flutter open.

Their eyes clashed. Her gaze was dewy, sleepy, and Julian's muscles tensed as he waited for her to speak up, praying her first words weren't "Put me down!"

He tightened his grip as he waited for the inevitable, but instead of kicking or screaming and demanding he release her, Molly hugged him even tighter and buried her face into his neck, where she quietly started sobbing.

The words tumbled out of his throat in an anxious rush. "Molly. Molly, I'm sorry. Don't cry. I'm sorry for what I said."

"No, Jules, I'm s-sorry, too. I—I overreacted, I—I'm s-so stupid. I should've known you anywhere. I should've known it was *you*."

Julian might have been considered a daredevil among

his sports friends, but seeing Molly cry just now tore up his insides.

He didn't think about what he was doing, only followed his instincts and carried her to his bedroom. He sat on the edge of his bed and clutched her quaking body to the exact place where his heart spasmed like an open wound inside his chest.

"I'm sorry, Molly. I should've brought it up and at least apologized," he said, smoothing his hands down her shivering back.

Her chest heaved as she sighed and stayed buried against his throat. "No, no, it was me. How could I not have known...not have *realized?*" She sniffled and glanced up, her eyes wide and blue and glazed with emotion. "At first I thought it was you, but then I felt his ring pressing against my arm. Why were you wearing it? Why didn't you tell me?"

"Baby, I thought you knew it was me that night. I thought you responded because it was *me*. I was going to leave you alone, Molly, but you called me back onto the terrace and I couldn't stop myself."

He had a similar sensation now as he marveled at the incredible feel of her in his arms, warm and shivering and vulnerable, like she'd been that night, ravenous for his mouth and his touches. He wanted to protect her, possess her, claim her, love her, make her never ever think again of anyone but him.

Cradling her face, he wiped her tears with the pads of his thumbs. "Why would you think it was Garrett, Molly? Don't you see the way I look at you? The way I want you? Everyone around us has noticed but you. Do you believe I'd help another man, *any* man, get even a little piece of you, when I've been waiting all my life to claim you as mine?"

She looked into his face, and her eyes widened at his

words, as though she'd only just realized that he *wanted* her. Her hands trembled as she cupped the back of his head, and then she kissed him. Softly. Whispering against his lips, "I love you. I'd die if I lost you, Jules. I'd rather lose my arms and never paint again than lose you."

Her lips pressed lightly against his, the words, the touch sending a shock of awareness bolting through his system. He stiffened under her, his heart kicking full speed, pumping hard and loud as a jolt of arousal coursed through his bloodstream.

When she drew back, her eyes shone like beacons, and the blatant desire he saw in those blue, blue eyes could've toppled him to his knees.

He was having trouble getting a word out, his arms shaking as he palmed her face between his open hands. "Do you want me?" he finally rasped.

His lips tingled from her sweet kiss, and now his mouth burned with the hunger to plunder her lips. Ripe with innocence, wet and pink and waiting to unleash all her passion on him. He needed to make her his. Only his. He couldn't bear another night, another second, another moment of his life without this.

He splayed his fingers across her scalp and gazed into her eyes in the shadows, so intoxicated with her nearness, he could only murmur in a thick whisper, "Do you want me, Molly? Do you want to be with me?" He slid his fingers down her back to palm the round curves of her buttocks, gently pulling her closer.

She nodded, struggling for air.

He gripped her hair within his fists and pinned her in place as he swept down. "I need to kiss you, touch you, make love to you." He fitted his lips perfectly to hers. His tongue plowed, swift and fast, into the warmth of her open mouth, and the pleasure of connection was so intense, a riptide of sensations racked his entire body.

She felt familiar and at the same time exotic and intoxicating to him. She was marshmallows in fire, lollipops under the covers, the best memories of his youth…she was museums, Monaco, fine wine….

She was Molly.

His lovely, effervescent Molly.

And he'd loved her almost as long as he'd been alive.

His arms snaked out to guide her legs around his hips, and suddenly she was straddling him, almost weightless, but burning hot and moving in restless excitement against him, her hands gliding up the bare muscles of his torso, her mouth ravenous on his. "Jules," she murmured. "Jules, I'm sorry for what I said."

"Shh, I'm sorry, too. Let's just forgive each other. You're mine, Molly, and I can't wait to be inside you." He twirled his tongue around hers, her body eagerly rocking over his hardness. Agonizing pleasure ripped through him as her weight bounced seductively over his straining erection.

Things went from slow to urgent in a heartbeat.

He anxiously unbuttoned her shirt, and when she started doing it herself, his hands slid up to caress her face. Panting fast and hard, he stroked her reddened bottom lip with alternating thumbs, her lovely jaw cradled within his cupped palms. He'd never seen so much desire in a woman's eyes. So much emotion. Her lips were so luscious, plump and damp and so unbelievably swollen from his kiss.

Desire pumped, hot and heady, through his bloodstream as he laid her down on the bed and pushed off his drawstring pants, licking her calves, her knees, touching her, looking at her—he couldn't get enough, do it quick enough, couldn't see her naked fast enough.

He wanted to part her slim, white thighs and taste her

honey. He wanted to make her gasp and moan and thrash against him as he introduced her to the greatest pleasures in the world. He was cooking inside of his body and he hadn't even started to do everything he wanted to. He had never thought he could want a woman like this.

He wanted to revere her. Adore her.

Molly was just as desperate, her fingers somehow cramping on the last buttons of her shirt. "I can't get this thing off. Please get it off, get it off, Jules!"

He cursed under his breath and lunged forward. He was being ripped in two from so much desire, so much rapture. He could barely speak from the euphoria, his fingers working as fast as they could through the tremors already shaking him.

"Is this mine? Is this an old shirt of mine?"

She nodded, and he swiftly grabbed it in both fists and tore it open, buttons flying everywhere. His blood roared like a monster in his ears when he parted the material, revealing flawless creamy skin he wanted to devour until tomorrow.

"Is this what you want, Molly?" He ducked to put his mouth on a beaded nipple that thrust up in the air. He laved it thoroughly as he rolled her to her side and sprawled his body right next to her as his hands engulfed the round curves of her buttocks and he drew her tighter against him, enabling him to feast on her breast like a man possessed.

She arched up against him as he twirled his tongue around the protruding tip, her whispers tickling his hair, "Yes, oh, please!"

He groaned, because he could never deny her. *Never.* He wanted her to be certain she wanted him and only him, as a man and as a lover, but she felt so right, was hot and lusty in his arms, in his bed, where he'd spent many sleepless nights as he imagined her lying in her own bed just next door.

No. He couldn't stop if he'd wanted to. For the first time in his life, he would be truly making love with someone.

Heart pounding at what was about to happen, something irrevocable, monumental, something he'd thought about his whole life, Julian turned her onto her back, his hands roaming down her curvy body, squeezing her lovely thighs as he kissed her long and languorously. "I want you. I need you. You feel so perfect. It's like coming home."

Her red hair splayed over his white down pillows. Her chest rose and fell heavily with each breath, her eyes so trusting he could drown in them. "I'm still a virgin, Jules." She reached out to stroke his dampened lips with one fingertip.

He placed a kiss on the tip of that fingertip. "Sweet, sweet baby, you have no idea what knowing that does to me." He was so honored, so turned on that he would be her first, her only. His hands shook as he eased the shirt off her shoulders and helped her pull it off her arms. "I'll be extra careful, but you have to tell me if I ever go too fa— Oh, Molly, *look at you*."

His eyes blurred at the sight of her completely naked. Her slim legs, her tiny hips, the little thatch of red curls at the apex of her thighs, and the two perfect globes of her breasts staring back at him, large and round, with those perky pink nipples that begged to be laved and licked and loved until morning.

She drew his hand up to one large globe, her eyes holding his with such innocent seduction he could've wept. His body trembled with anticipation, excitement.

"Do you want me to kiss you here again?" he gruffly said, and cupped both her breasts in his big hands, gently squeezing. She shivered in pleasure when he began teasing the pink areolae with his thumbs.

He bent his head and took one firm bud between his lips. He flicked it with his tongue first, then drew it deeply into his mouth as his hand trailed down her stomach. She gasped under him. Her hips rolled enticingly as his fingers teased through her moistness.

"You're so damp," he rasped, watching her expression melt as he eased one finger gently inside her. "And so damned tight you're going to make me come before I even get started."

Her honey pooled in his hand as her entry snugly enclosed his penetrating finger. Restless and mewing softly, she arched up on the bed and pressed her breast to his mouth. He suckled her with a growl of pleasure and plunged a second finger inside her.

Her soft moan tumbled into the air, and her hips rocked against his hand in silent plea. He drew back, panting, and met her blue gaze, an ocean of arousal, her lashes heavy, her mouth red, her nipples red…

Undone, he slid down her body and buried his head between her legs, giving her a hungry kiss that penetrated her to her sweet, warm depths. She cried out and pulled helplessly on his hair. "Stop, oh, please stop or you'll make me…"

He lifted his head. Urgency thrummed through his body like a living, breathing thing. He was panting, drowning in ecstasy, in his need to make it special and memorable for her while at the same time trying to withhold his body's natural reactions to tonight. To being with her after wanting her for so long.

"I'll make you what?" he prodded softly, coming up and brushing his nose against hers. "Do you already want to come?"

She nodded, her breath fast and hot against his face.

He wanted to take those breaths and suck them into his body, to take this woman and mark her with his touch, every inch of her, for eternity. Catching her bottom lip between his and gently suckling, he caressed her between the legs again. "But that's a good thing…"

She plunged her hands into his hair and set a kiss on his lips, the tip of his nose, his square jaw. "Not alone—Jules, please. When it happens, I want to feel you inside me. I've always wondered what it… I've been dying to feel this…"

Her fingers delved between their bodies, and he almost yelped at the incredible feel, the amazing feel, of her hand curling around his hard length as if she owned him. "I want you," she breathed, her eyes wide in surprise at what she touched. "I…I want *this*…" She stroked his full length exploratively, and a barrage of pleasure raced through his system. He bit back an oath as his body instantly tensed for release.

He grabbed her wrists and playfully pinned her arms up over her head, then he dived to give her a hot, ravenous kiss on the lips. "If you do that again we won't get to the part of me actually entering you."

She writhed underneath him, her breasts beckoning another kiss. "Please, please."

He was unraveled by her desire, enchanted by her openness to him, his undeniable connection to her. His hands shook with male-hormone overload as he reached out to the nightstand.

He briskly rolled on a condom as fast as he could. Realizing she'd been watching in fascination, he pushed her back down with his weight and reached for both her creamy ankles. He couldn't wait to be inside her. Feel her heat.

Make her mine, mine, mine.

"Do you want me inside you…?" he urged as he hooked her legs around his hips, his pulse fluttering like crazy.

"Please, yes. Oh…" She gasped as he penetrated her, firm and slow, pushing in inch by inch, her tender body fighting him. The effort it took to hold back made his every muscle quiver in restraint.

"Ahh, I'm sorry, this is going to hurt you…"

She'd gone motionless beneath him, those trusting, wide eyes clawing at his heart as she clasped his shoulders in a death grip. "Don't tense against me, don't fight me," he cooed, easing back to let her breathe, then carefully guiding himself back in, caressing her nipple tips to incite her relaxation as he gently rocked his hips. "Give yourself to me, Molly. Be mine."

He thumbed the little pearl above the entry of her sex, and he felt her give him another inch, and another, until he was almost buried to the hilt. Suddenly, with fierce determination, Molly thrust her pelvis up against him and they both cried out in surprise—he barked in pleasure, and she moaned in sudden pain, and they both went utterly still, completely joined, his length pulsing inside her, her body snugly wrapped around him.

He took her breathless little mouth and kissed her fiercely as the compact heat of her body adjusted to his length. Struggling to hold back, his heart thundering in his chest, he threw his head back in ecstasy and finally started to withdraw, enjoying every sliding inch. "So good. You feel so. *Good.*" He bent down and kissed her, a hot, wild kiss. "Please stay still, baby, I don't want to hurt you."

He went back in, and she moaned in pleasure, her fingers clenching his buttocks, urging him on. "It's okay now. It's okay. Don't hold back, Julian."

"Oh, Molly…you have no idea what you've been doing to me…." He rocked his hips gently against hers, the mo-

tion slow but deep and incredibly erotic. Excruciating pleasure shot through his system as he continued his rhythmic
thrusting, waiting to feel her shudder, waiting for her to
come apart in his arms.

Suddenly, their eyes locked, and Molly released an out-
of-control moan, her nails biting into his skin as she arched
up in pleasure.

She watched him watch her.

She felt like crying, dying, flying.

She thought she'd break when he first entered her, and
now the pleasure had overridden anything else.

Julian's eyes were an inferno of passion, eating her up
alive. His hands slid like satin on her skin, over her hips,
her rib cage, caressing her breasts. Then he ducked his
head once more and his velvet tongue branded every inch
of her body until every cell and atom felt alive and fevered.

A sheen of perspiration clung to his forehead, and she
ached to lick it up and get drunk on him. High on him.
She thrashed under his eyes when their gazes met, glory-
ing in the ravaged way he looked at her, the tender words
that tumbled off his lips as he took her, words like *adore*
and *want you* and *killing me*.

Inside her being, she overflowed with love for him.
Him. She wanted all of him, all of Julian John Gage, as
she watched his muscles flexing hard with each move of
his powerful body against hers.

And when his rhythm turned erratic, her eyes drifted
shut and the passion overtook her. She clutched his bulging
shoulders with a soft cry of pure, unrefined bliss, hearing
him let loose a growl of his own, and they snapped and
twisted together, clutching each other, tense and shaking,
and then…seconds later…slumping, relaxed and entwined,
they felt as if they were one, at last.

* * *

They couldn't get enough of each other.

After less than two hours of sleep, Molly awakened to find Julian's tousled blond head trailing suspiciously down her tummy and heading south, his fingertips sensuously playing between her splayed thighs. Drawing out her wetness, he made her mew in her throat and toss her head back helplessly against the pillow.

When he buried his face in the damp, warm place where his fingers had been, she gripped the sheets at her sides as each hot flick of his knowing tongue set a rampage of sensations loose in her body. She arched and twisted. "Jules, please…" she gasped in the dark. He pushed her to a climax with his tongue, and then he wrapped her legs around his hips and rode her until she was crying out to him in ecstasy.

Less than an hour later, she stirred in bed and searched for his warmth, having somehow been separated from him during sleep. She hooked one leg around his narrow hips and draped her arm around his waist, and as she wiggled to get comfortable, she became aware of the large, prominent erection biting into her hip bone. She stilled, but Julian had already awakened. He groaned and dropped his head in search of her lips in the shadows, and she gave her mouth up to his. Lying on their sides on the bed, he entered her slowly, whispering sweet little nothings in her ears that drove her to a climax that left her gasping for breath and blushing over all the things he said.

They showered together and laughed over "bun-buns" and "JJ," then returned to bed. Then, at 5:00 a.m., while a tiny stream of light filtered through the closed drapes, Molly once again woke up to find herself entangled in Julian's muscled limbs and his Egyptian cotton bedsheets. She couldn't seem go back to sleep. She throbbed all over in such a delicious way. Adrenaline and excitement continued coursing through her system, and she couldn't stop touching him. Kissing him. Smelling his skin, which smelled clean and of his sandalwood soap.

"Jules," she whispered, going breathless at the excitement of waking up with him. "Are you asleep?"

"Not anymore." With an arm draped over his eyes as he lay sprawled on the bed, Julian's chest rose and fell with each breath, his voice groggy and sexy.

Molly sat up and edged closer, waiting for him to stir to action. "I'm still naked," she said, dropping her voice to a seductive purr.

Dropping his arm and cracking his eyes open, Julian stroked his thumb down the length of her arm, his expression deadly serious. "I know what you're begging for, Molls."

Before she could even blink, he'd rolled her over with a lionlike "rawr" that made her squeal and laugh her heart out as he gave her the tickle torture of her life. "Oh, I hate it when you do this, stop it, *stop!*" she squealed in between hysterical laughs, but he didn't pause for a whole half a minute—because it wasn't called torture for nothing. They ended up breathless and grinning from ear to ear when it was finally over.

He turned somber as he gazed down at her flushed features, then he reached out to cup her naked breast and manipulate it as though it were his property to play with. When her nipple responded eagerly, his smile turned wolfish, and a devilish glint appeared in his gaze.

"You sure you can take me?" he said, and bent his head to give her a leisurely good-morning kiss, his seductive lips stirring her senses. "I don't want you hurting all day."

She was still breathless from his torture. "Well, I do."

He laughed. "What an insatiable little devil my little

Molls is turning out to be." He smiled that wolf's smile again, his eyes spelling mischief, then he ducked his blond head and playfully nipped the beaded points of her nipples, and the stimulus was almost too much to bear.

"Thank you for the gift you've given me," he whispered against her flesh, switching from one nipple to the other. "My entire life I worried someone else would take what I wanted."

That husky, unexpected confession turned her on like flicking on a light switch, and together with the nibbles he was giving her? It was a winning combo. Her muscles stiffened as the blissful sensations rippled through her. She clung to his shoulders, squirming as red-hot desire took her over and his warm, wet tongue tortured her beyond measure.

"Oh, Jules," she sighed. "Don't do that unless you... you know."

"Yeah, I know," he said, coming up to her ear, murmuring, "I got you, baby, you know I do."

Molly turned her head, opened her mouth and kissed him, lazily at first, then vigorously. "No. Now it's my turn to torture you," she said sheepishly.

She pushed him under her and he obediently lay on his back as she greedily took in his magnificent body with her eyes. From head to toe, Julian was a masterpiece she wanted to memorize.

Eyes narrowed, he crossed his hands behind his head and let her touch him, like a pasha being pampered and tended to. She bit her bottom lip while her breasts throbbed for his touch and the place between her legs pricked with wanting. Her hands stroked his abs and pectorals and round, hard biceps, and then trailed downward to cup his mesmerizing hardness....

He sucked in a harsh breath through his teeth. Molly's

eyes blurred as she seized his hard length—so big she could not grip him with only one hand. He was so aroused and powerful that she could feel him pulsing underneath her palms and fingers. She wanted to lick him there, lick him everywhere, like a lollipop. "I want to kiss you here, Jules." She patted him gently, her insides clenching with pure, unadulterated lust.

His nostrils flared, his eyes almost black. "Then stop teasing and kiss me."

Molly watched his face as she bent her head, and she would never forget the flaming, pulse-pounding lust in his eyes, as if he could eat her up and not want anything else for the rest of his life. "Like this?" she asked tentatively as she dipped her puckered lips and placed a kiss right on the tip.

His hips bucked wildly, his biceps bulging as he fought to keep his arms back.

"Do you like it, Jules, or—?"

"Baby, I've dreamed of this," he murmured in a coarse, thick voice, his torso rising and falling with each soughing breath. "Morning, noon and night, I've dreamed of this…."

Molly bent her head and watched him, melting in heat at the harsh look of ecstasy on his face. His eyes burned into the top of her head as she snaked out her tongue to lick him in a slow circle around the tip, savoring his taste and the incredible feel of his hardness sliding into her mouth. She opened wider and took the first couple of inches inside of her. His hands rounded over the back of her head and his fingertips delved gently into her hair as he eased her head back so their gazes locked. Her eyes felt heavy with arousal, and his gaze was thick-lashed and stormy.

"Did you think of me, too, baby?" he said in a guttural whisper, and Molly released him, then climbed on top of him and straddled his hips, bending to press her lips hungrily to his.

"So much I've never even looked at another man, Jules," she whispered into his mouth.

She felt the powerful tremor that rushed through his body at her words. Then he took charge and twirled his tongue around hers while his hands slid down her back to grip her buttocks. He squeezed the plump flesh, moving her so their hips aligned and his rigid erection pressed right into the part where she was soaked.

"I've thought of this every day for so damned long. I won't even begin to tell you how many times during the night."

"I want you in me, Jules." She rocked her hips enticingly against his length. She was wonderfully sore and yet needed to feel him again, only to be sure this was real. This was happening. She was his, and he was hers.

Hard and strong, he easily rolled her over and loomed above her now, and the sight of him poised at her entry drove her to the edge. His golden skin glowed with a thin sheen of perspiration, and his shoulders and arms bulged with straining muscles, corded with pumping veins. She couldn't believe that this wonderful creature would want her like he did. Would look at her in the way he was looking down at her now. That her hero and friend and favorite person in the world could also be her lover.

Clutching him closer, she whispered, "I want you, but slowly so it won't hurt."

"I'll be careful with you. Come here, Moo." He gathered her closer, holding her firmly against him as he slowly eased inside her.

"Yes!" she cried out, squeezing her eyes shut against the onslaught of sensation—a deluge of love and passion and everything she'd always wanted. Right here in her arms, after years of being so close to it.

A sound tore from his straining body as he began a hard, thorough pace, his lips dragging wildly over her face, her lips, her cheeks, her temple as his hips rammed against hers and she held on to him for dear life. He drove her to the precipice and made her gasp out his name, and then he followed her with one last thrust, her body clutching his in a long, tight orgasm.

For an hour afterward they lay entangled in bed and re- membered their little adventures as teenagers. As Molly drifted off to sleep, she felt so content, so genuinely happy, she thought at last her life was as it should be.

Nothing would come between her and her soul mate any longer.

Eight

Full sunlight streamed through the windows of Julian's bedroom as Molly cracked open one eye, and then the other. Noticing it was past 10:00 a.m., she moaned languorously and rolled and stretched on the bed, anxious to feel the warm contours of the body she'd snuggled against all night long. But Julian wasn't in bed with her.

Disappointment swept through her as she sat up. Then she spotted the note over his pillow, and she instantly relaxed.

> Good morning, Picasso. Meet me upstairs? Business is ready to open Monday and I'm giving it a thorough check. Hope you don't mind I left another message for you somewhere.
> Yours,
> Julian

The other message, it turned out, was right on her left buttock. Molly gasped when she caught sight of it as she passed by the mirror. It consisted of three red letters, perfectly curved, perfectly marking her fanny like a cattle brand, except he'd used her paint: *JJG.*

She laughed so hard that tears popped into her eyes. She'd never imagined she could wake up feeling so content, so full, so complete, so happy. How could she have spent all these years next to this man she would give her life for, and miss out on all of *this?*

It was as though last night Jules had opened the little box where she'd hidden away entire decades of special, secret feelings for him, and now that those feelings were out, Molly feared she'd burst from the love in her chest.

Scrambling to catch up with him, she showered and found herself drifting off to last night as she shampooed. They'd lain awake remembering stuff about their childhood, then they'd laughed, then their laughter had faded into heat once more, and they'd kissed and made out and made love until they'd exploded.

Hot and bothered by the memory alone, she jumped out of the shower, wrapped herself in a towel and rushed to the walk-in closet to survey her clothes. She settled on a short white jean skirt and a lacy white blouse. Then she fixed coffee and folded two warm croissants she'd heated in the oven into a pair of napkins. She carried the croissants and the two coffee mugs up in the elevator, watching them steam with a smile.

She could too easily picture doing this every day, too easily imagine having her husband's offices in the same building as her apartment. He could come and go as he pleased—take a few moments in his busy day to steal away between meetings and come home and kiss her. Kiss her heart out like at that masquerade, like last night, like, hopefully, later this morning. Her cheeks flamed at the prospect.

The elevator chimed and she stepped out, impressed by the sight that greeted her.

Wow.

The place had undergone a huge transformation. She hadn't noticed all this last night when she'd been painting like a fiend. But now full sunlight streamed through the windows, and every inch of the marble floor sparkled clean. Chrome chandeliers hung from the rafters, brand-new computers sat proudly atop their shiny new desks. A main reception desk stood before her, and behind it, the wall of her partly finished mural said a cheery good morning.

Just looking at that explosion of colors made her anxious to work on it some more. But the truth was, she was feverish to see Julian. Her breasts pricked at the thought of kissing his silken lips and wrapping herself around his big, hard body again....

She heard voices then. Angry voices.

Frowning, she went around the wall through a set of glass doors. And that was when she spotted Julian. Beautiful in khaki slacks and a white polo short, his casual weekend clothes. But there was nothing casual in his wide stance, in his massively tense shoulders, the arms that strained at his sides.

And then she saw the second man, his stance as menacing as Julian's.

Garrett.

Molly's heart stopped.

Her eyes wildly searched Julian's profile for clues. He looked more than furious. His nostrils were flaring, and though the movements were almost imperceptible, he kept flexing his fingers as though they were cramping. Or as though he was just aching to throttle someone.

O-oookay. This might just not be the morning she had envisioned while she was taking a shower. What were they arguing about anyway? And why was Garrett here if he didn't know about Julian's new—

Oh, no.

No, no, no.

All of a sudden it hit her. And she feared that she knew exactly what the two men were arguing about.

Her own words came back to haunt her like a curse.

"Who the hell can even work in peace with this sort of constant criticism? I'm glad he's ready to move on!"

Oh, no, please no.

Garrett had sounded less than thrilled when he'd demanded to know if Julian was leaving. She swayed nervously on her feet and a wash of hot coffee spilled across her left wrist. Pain shot up her arm, and when she gasped, both men turned.

She locked gazes with Garrett first, somehow avoiding Julian's gaze out of dread. She didn't want to know if he was angry. Not after the incredible, mesmerizing night they had spent together. But really, how angry could he be? He was naturally an easygoing man and would probably take it well and laugh about it later. It wasn't as if she had revealed super top secret information, had she? *Had she?*

She breathed out slowly and smiled at the window behind their shoulders. "I didn't know we had company, Jules."

"I find that hard to believe, somehow, since you issued the invitation."

Her heart skipped a beat when she heard his voice; it was low and silky as a ribbon, but it was the winter coolness of the tone that made the hairs on the back of her neck stand up in alarm. Her eyes jerked to lock with his, and for a moment she needed to recover from the utter slamming force of his accusing gaze.

"Jules," she said, slowly tossing her hair from side to side. "I didn't invite him here. I did not mean for him to… Uh, here, you can take my coffee, Garrett, if you'd like."

She extended a mug, trying once again to turn this crazy morning around to the morning she wanted. The one she'd dreamed of. If Garrett took the hospitable offering, Julian would have to take the second one and maybe after the croissants they'd all—

"Already bringing coffee to the love of your life, Molly? Too bad he was just leaving. Aren't you, brother?"

Once again, Molly's eyebrows furrowed in confusion over Julian's frigid tone. For a dazed moment, she almost expected Julian to chuckle and admit he was teasing her. Like he did when he dared her to wear that wench costume or asked her to kiss his six-pack and go as low as she would go in the darkened office at Landon's house.

But no laughter followed his words.

"What the hell are you talking about?" Garrett burst out.

Molly realized in dawning horror that Julian had referred to Garrett as the love of her life. She glanced down at the mugs both men had refused and the sticky residue of coffee on her wrist, growing numb in disbelief. Had he been making fun of her having stupidly thought she loved Garrett once upon a time, or did he actually believe it to be *true?*

Drawing in a steadying breath, she walked around and shakily set the mugs and croissants on a nearby desk. A little part of her already wanted to get hysterical, but she tried reminding herself that, although she'd spoken out impulsively, the last thing she'd intended was to harm Julian.

She would have time to explain all of this in a couple of minutes, just a few minutes more....

"Please tell me you're having someone check your goddamned head because you're not making any sense," Garrett thundered, then he turned to her. "Thanks for your visit yesterday, Molly," he said. "And for keeping us in the loop of this development."

Molly froze. She could not even believe he would say that to her in front of Julian. Seriously, she'd never expected things to go south so fast. Suddenly, she trembled with the fantastical urge to fling the coffee mugs at Garrett's face for ruining what should've been a perfect morning, for now there was no doubt whatsoever that Julian would believe she had been a little snitch who had betrayed his confidence and trust.

God. It sounded so bad now that she reflected on it, and yet she wouldn't have even said it at all if they hadn't infuriated her so on Julian's behalf!

Instead of giving Garrett any sort of answer, she pursed her lips and pretended to be super busy sucking the spilled coffee from her left wrist. Garrett had spoken the words in true gratitude, maybe even with a bit of tenderness, but she still loathed the fact that Julian had found out that her mouth had apparently gotten ahead of her brain yesterday.

Garrett sighed and turned to Julian, his timbre hardening. "Think about it, before you do something even stupider," he said, and walked toward the reception area and out to the elevators.

Molly finished sucking up the coffee and suddenly felt too energetic, as if she needed to do something. Parachute, river raft, hike Mount Everest? Artists were solitary people by nature, too emotional, too vulnerable, too incapable of handling awfulness like this. Fighting to stand still, she frantically counted the seconds after Garrett left that Julian remained silent. Just watching her. So very, very silent.

Fifty.

Fifty hellish seconds.

While Molly wanted to hide under the chair, blend with her mural or just scream.

Because she was just coming to realize how big a mistake she'd made. She'd done something very wrong to him. Very, very wrong.

Jules didn't trust anyone. Anyone but *her.* Oh, God, now his family would be riding him hard about coming back. Maybe they couldn't send him away like they used to when they were displeased with him, but did she dare wonder how they could pressure him to bend to their united wills?

What had she just *done* to him?

With a pounding heart, she waited for him to speak, every second eternal, miserable. The top two buttons of his polo shirt were unbuttoned. He wore the masquerade ring on his hand. His fingers were curling and uncurling into fists at his sides.

She wanted to die.

"You ratted me out to my brother."

He spoke softly. Too softly. Way too softly.

She sucked in a breath, surprised by the pain cutting through her rib cage. If he'd said, *You suck. You're a liar. Last night was a mistake,* it might have hurt less. Shame spread through her like wildfire. Because how had she not seen this coming? "It's not how it looks, Jules," she told him, but his expression was so harsh and scary her gaze dipped once more to the floor.

His shoes were so polished and shiny. Were they advancing toward her?

He turned her face up to his with his thumb and forefinger, forcing her to look into his piercing eyes. "You ratted me out to my brother, Molly. How the hell could you do this to me?"

Just to stand there under the searing heat of his reproachful green stare made her empty stomach churn. "I didn't mean to! It slipped. *It slipped.* What? Are you going to hate me now, is that it?"

"Hate? Molly, I freaking *love* you! I can't believe you'd line up with them against me." He raked his hands through his hair and then backed away, as though she had a rash he needed to distance himself from. "You want to know why I would leave a thriving, billion-dollar business, Molly? Fine, let me tell you why. Because as long as I'm under my family's thumb, I'll never be able to be with you."

His expression was grim as he watched her, his eyebrows drawn sharp and sullen over his eyes; eyes that killed her with emotion as he looked at her.

"That day you came to me begging me to help you get another man…I thought to *hell* with my family. I wasn't going to let them ruin my life anymore and let them keep me away from you, Moo."

Molly incongruously wondered why Julian could say *Moo* and make it sound revered and womanly, sexy and beautiful, but she was so distraught over the rest of what he said that she didn't wonder for long. Julian's face had hardened with pain and his voice felt like icicles on her skin. Molly's eyes had blurred with tears because each and every one of the words he'd said was eating her up inside.

"They've sent me away dozens of times, they've threatened to disown me, they've tried every twisted plot to keep me in line. And I'm sick and tired of dancing to their tune. I just want to be with *you*." His green eyes clawed her like talons as he spread his arms out, his jaw clenched so tight she feared it would crack like her heart was cracking. "So this was the plan. This was my plan. With my full financial independence, I'll need no one—no one—to tell me what to do, or tell me if I can or can't love you, Molly. Dammit, I can't freaking believe you'd crucify me for them—*for him.*"

He pulled at the collar of his polo shirt as if he wanted to rip it off him and then stalked to the floor-to-ceiling window. Molly mourned his affection already. No more sparkling green eyes. There were only tornadoes and storms now.

And she'd put them there.

A tear slipped down her cheek as her brain replayed his words over and over in her head, then a second tear followed, and a third, and they wouldn't stop. Julian *loved* her. Oh, God. To know that he'd cared for her all this time, had wanted her like she'd secretly wanted him and had been actually doing something so he could be with her…

To know the truest kind of love could have been hers all along…

This should have been the happiest day of her life. But instead it had morphed into the worst.

Because to learn that you had something on the same day you lost it *sucked.*

Molly wanted to tear her skin off with her nails, her heart out with her hands so she could show him all she wanted was to give it to him. "I'm sorry, Jules," she said, clutching her stomach. "I didn't know it was so important. I swear I would have watched my mouth better—"

"I trusted you, Molly," he interrupted, shaking his head over and over again. "You know me better than my family, better than anyone. I've trusted you with everything. Everything I think and want, and… Jesus, I just can't do this right now."

He put even more distance between them and jammed his fingers into his hair as each step carried him farther away.

"You can still trust me, Jules! I was careless, that's all. I mean…you're not going to let Garrett push you into anything you don't want to do. Are you?"

He halted. And she trembled at the expression on his face, so…vacant, as if not only would he never, ever trust her again, but neither would he care to try.

This steely detachment on his part was so new and alarming, when he turned to face the window and gave her a view of his broad, impenetrable back, she actually wanted to flee to her studio and lock herself up the rest of her life in a sanctuary of paint, brushes and blank canvases.

But her life would never be the same without him, would never be the same if she didn't stay here and work things out. Julian was, quite simply, the most valuable and treasured thing in the world to her.

He *had* to forgive her.

So she remained. She remained glued to the floor, to this present, this horrible alternate reality where Julian looked at her as a…fraud.

"Jules?" she prodded when he remained staring silently out the window for too long.

He ran a hand all the way through his hair and gripped the back of his neck, then stared down at the floor. "Was I your consolation prize, Molly? Do you still have…an idea of you and Garrett in your head?"

She opened her mouth to deny it, but only heard a shocked gasp, the question so terribly painful to hear. Did he not realize she *adored* him? Did he think she would spend a night like last night just for the *fun* of it?

"If it had been Garrett kissing you that night at the masquerade, for real, would you even be here with me, Molly? Or would you have left here with him?" he asked, and when he dropped his arm and turned slightly, his empty stare slashed her to bits.

How could he think that?

She wanted to hit him for even thinking it, but she felt shattered inside.

The magic she'd felt in that kiss could never have been there with Garrett or anyone else. It was him, Julian, it always had been, no matter how much she'd tried to fight it. He was The One.

Him and only him.

But she couldn't speak. To her frustration, she was crying now, and with her throat so tight, it was really hard to get a word out.

She'd never imagined she could ever hurt anyone. She loved to laugh, to enjoy life, to paint. She was young at heart and had never seen herself as a threat to anyone— not even to a bug, because she had a habit of escorting them out to the yard and never squashing a single one. She would cut out her eyes for Julian if he needed them, her hands so she could never paint again. She'd give him two kidneys, her liver, and her pancreas and lungs, too! She wouldn't even mention her heart because she'd never really had it to herself in the first place.

She'd given it along with her lollipop to a six-year-old boy a long, long time ago.

"Julian, don't be ridiculous, please. I love you," she said as she wiped her tears, rushing after him when he'd got tired of waiting for her to reply. But he was already boarding the elevator, as proud and stubborn as all the Gage men she'd ever known.

"Get your stuff, Molly. I'm taking you back home. Consider the mural done."

Nine

For exactly twelve days, eleven hours, forty-seven minutes and thirty-two seconds, Julian buried himself in work, sweat and sports. He hadn't set foot at the *San Antonio Daily* in almost two weeks. Not even to present his damned brothers with his resignation letter.

No. Since then, JJG Enterprises had officially opened for business, so instead he'd buried himself in work from 6:00 a.m. to 6:00 p.m. each day, and after that he had been rowing, paddling, kayaking, running, climbing and sky-diving his freaking heart out.

He would come home at midnight, soaked in sweat, to feed his body, bathe himself and drop down dead on the bed. But it was no use. His head continued swimming with memories of making love to Molly, kissing her sweet lips. Memories of her betrayal.

He'd never thought that a casual, collected guy like

him, with everything under control, would ever get to feel that way.

And every day when he saw her mural upstairs, he wanted to tear that wall down. It was so bright and vivid, so sassy, so Molly. He could bulldoze it to the ground if he didn't have millions invested up there. Millions. Hell, his whole damned heart, since he'd imagined sharing that future with Molly.

Now he didn't even want to wake up.

Even his home, once his sanctuary, seemed to assault him with memories at every turn.

Her scent lingered in the pillows. He kept finding her stuff around the house. Fashion magazines. A random paintbrush. In the kitchen pantry he'd find the artificial sweetener she claimed was the best sitting right next to the honey he liked to gobble. And those damned Sleepytime Teas.

He hadn't realized until the glaring emptiness of life without Molly stared him in the face every day how deeply she had infiltrated his life. She had been involved, in little and big ways, in every part of his day. From the cookies he'd snack on at the office or at home, provided by Molly from Kate's delicious kitchen, to the text messages reminding him of a family gathering to her calls—*Forget to say hi yesterday, moron? Call me. Or else!*

He wanted to forget he'd ever met this woman, forget he'd ever wanted her, forget he'd been prepared to change his whole life around for her....

But he couldn't.

He couldn't forgive her. If only he could just forget her. Forget the way she laughed with him, at him, and poked and prodded him and made his body feel alive in a way nobody else did. He'd had strings of lovers but had never enjoyed sex so much, cherished the moment so fiercely as that night he'd spent with her.

He'd replayed it in his head dozens of times, groaning and suffering like a masochist, but the reality had been so sweet he didn't want to forget that time with her. Ever. To have finally seen her, sprawled and wanting him in his bed, that red hair fanning across his sheets, could still give a grown man wet dreams.

She'd said she loved him a thousand times in her life. He knew she did. As a friend. As a "brother." But did she *love* him? Julian had been inside her, knew every secret of her body, knew where to press her, how to make her moan, what she ate, what she feared, where to tickle her. Would she rather have spent that night with Garrett?

Garrett.

His blood boiled at the thought of his brother. Even though he knew Molly's feelings for Garrett had been based on a kiss that Julian himself had given her, he continued to feel so jealous he couldn't even see straight. He couldn't believe that she would betray him to his brother like she had. So *why* had she?

Had two decades of pure, raw friendship meant nothing to her?

He desperately tried fishing his memories for clues of her and his brother together. Looks he could've missed. Touches that had more weight to them than they should have. But he came up with nothing. Every memory of Molly was tied to one man, and that man was *him*. Maybe he had not always been a man. But when he had been a boy, he had been *her* boy.

Jules, Jules, gimme a piggyback ride.

And when Kate had tried to patch her up after a good scrape and would coo down at Molly in a maternal way, "I'm going to kiss your boo-boo better," little Molly would point at Julian across the room and grin. "No, I want him to do it."

And later, as teens: *Teach me to surf, Jules. Will you drive me over to art class, Jules?*

And as an adult: *Coffee? Tea? Call me! I'm still alive, you know, just been painting!*

But now he was alone.

So damned alone.

Yeah, that was him.

The careless playboy with a broken heart.

The sun shone overhead so bright, Molly was surprised she didn't disintegrate like a vampire under its glare. After being locked in her studio for weeks, it was almost a miracle her skin did not instantly peel off from sunlight exposure. She might even deserve such a fate.

At least if you asked Julian, who, she assumed, wanted her dead.

Eyes narrowed to shield herself from some of the sun's brightness, she gazed down at the envelope she gripped in her clammy hands, recognizing the handwriting as that of Julian's assistant, Ms. Watts.

So. This is what their friendship and one-night stand—because truly, that was all they'd managed to have together—had come to.

Communicating through the post office.

She closed her mailbox and had to sit down on the grass next to the sidewalk and just stare down at that white envelope.

Her texts had not been answered.

Her calls went straight to voice mail.

She wanted to kill the jerk for being so silly and dramatic, and at the same time she wanted to slap herself for opening her big mouth to Garrett without thinking.

Julian was, and had always been, an extremely private man. He showed his cool and aloof side to everyone but only showed his true self to a select few. Molly knew, deep down, that no one knew Julian better than she did.

He couldn't stand to talk about politics but oh, he sure loved to steal her Lucky Charms marshmallows. He was a sports and sports-memorabilia fanatic, and if he was not a businessman, he'd probably spend all day doing water sports at the lake surfer, with his suntan and lazy charm and a wakeboard under him. He'd never felt as if he belonged in his family—never really felt as if he belonged anywhere.

And that was why she couldn't stand to remember what she'd unwittingly done to him.

He'd longed for freedom in his life, and instead she'd blown the whistle on him to his family so they could tie him back up and keep him from flying. She had done that. To the man she had constantly, throughout her life, loved in every way a woman could love a man.

The worst part of it was that Julian never let anyone in.

But Molly had always come in through the back door.

And he'd let her. Enjoyed it, even. Cared for her, protected her, coddled her.

And she'd accidentally betrayed him to a man whom he'd believed she wanted over him.

How could she ever make things right if he didn't even want to talk to her?

It had been fifteen days since she'd seen him now, and each day she'd tried to make amends. Her last attempt had been returning every penny of the money he'd wired to her for her unfinished mural. With a note that read, I've never left a work unfinished until now. Please give me a chance—I'd like to finish this.

She'd written a thousand notes before settling on that

one. Some had said, *I love you* and *please* and *forgive me*. But she'd been too much of a chicken to send any of those, and so she'd settled on the most businesslike one, thinking it was probably her best chance of getting an entry with him.

She drew a deep breath and peeled the envelope open with shaky fingers. The check she had written to him for the $150,000 fell into her open palm, shredded to pieces. There was no note. Except her own note. Shredded to pieces, as well.

She thought she heard her heart crack.

Her eyes welled with tears and she ducked her face when a car approached. Tires screeched, a motor shut down and doors opened.

Kate and Beth stepped out of the Catering, Canapés and Curry van. "Molly?" Kate said, alarmed.

Molly used her hair to shield her profile from view and jammed the pieces of the check and note back into the envelope, rising to her feet and quickly wiping at her cheeks. "Hey. I'll help you." She didn't look at them as she went to the back of the van and began unloading their empty trays, but she could feel their eyes on her as she headed inside the house.

Beth caught up with her in the kitchen. "Molly?"

Molly prayed to God her eyes weren't red, and even smiled as she set the trays down on the kitchen counter. "Hey, Beth."

She could see the concern in Beth's expression, and she feared that there was even a little pity there, too. "You know, Julian came by the house the other day. To speak to Landon. He resigned from the *Daily*."

Molly nodded as her airway constricted. "Good for him."

Beth studied her. Molly knew she was a good woman.

She had known heartache and a horrid divorce before she had found true love in her life, and suddenly Molly wanted to wail her heart out to her. Because surely this woman would understand how it felt when you were ripped apart, shredded like your notes and broken. But then Kate's heart would break for Molly if she saw her like this, and Molly didn't want to break her sister's heart.

It was her own fault that all this had happened. Kate had warned her so many times, so, so many times, about Julian. Maybe Molly had even had it coming.

"You know—" Beth grasped her hand and gave her an encouraging squeeze "—if it makes you feel any better, he's not doing too good, either."

Molly looked down at her bare toes, her chest heavy as if it were carrying the weight of a whole country. "It doesn't," she admitted, feeling like a bug as she remembered Julian's anger, his disappointment. The last thing she'd wanted was to make him suffer. "But thanks anyway, Beth."

That afternoon she went back to finishing the two canvases she had left for her exhibit at the Blackstone Gallery in New York. They ended up awful, tenebrous and depressing, reflecting her mood. But she still owed the gallery these two works, and because she had no time to start anew, they would have to do.

At night she lay in bed, her eyes dry as she heard Kate on the phone: "Not doing well… What are we going to do?"

Molly wanted to make a humble suggestion and tell her, and whomever she was talking to, to stay the hell away from her life, but then she just put her pillow over her face and groaned.

"Molly," Kate said from the door, a shaft of light entering with her.

"I heard you, Kate. I have ears, you know, and we don't

live in a mansion," she grumbled angrily, flinging the pillow aside.

The mattress squeaked as her sister sat by her side and took her hand. "I'm sorry, Moo. I think we've made a terrible mistake. With you and Julian, I mean."

"No. You were right all along." Molly rolled to her side and pulled her hand free to stick it under her cheek, suddenly rejecting any physical contact that didn't come from where she most craved it.

"Molly, we're planning something. Garrett, Landon, Beth and I. If I tell you what it is, will you go with it?"

"If it involves me lying again to anyone or pretending to be something I'm not, count me out."

"No, Moo, this is actually a good plan," Kate said, a smile in her voice. "All you'd really need to do is follow some instructions in a note that I'm going to give you this weekend. The note will lead you to Julian."

"I hate him."

"You do?"

"I've never met such a frustrating bastard in my life!"

"All right, then." The bed squeaked again as Kate got up to leave.

Molly sprang back up on the bed, her heart picking up speed as she switched on the lamp, and frantically blurted, "I was never really with him, Kate. It was all a lie. I was confused and thought that Garrett was the one who kissed me that night at the masquerade. I foolishly thought Julian could help me make Garrett jealous so he'd come around, but then I realized all along…"

Kate cocked her head from the doorway, her eyes brimming with understanding. "I know," she said. Coming back, she sat down and ran her hand down the length of Molly's hair. "Do you really think I believed that little act?

You two were so obviously not lovers I could've laughed if I hadn't been so very worried."

"But it was actually Julian who kissed me at the masquerade and I…I got mixed up. It was like my soul recognized him, but my brain *couldn't* or maybe didn't want to. All I know is that I needed to find this man and I needed to be with Julian while I did… It's his fault I can never look at other men, never want to be with anyone else. I even think I was pretending to want to make Garrett jealous but really wanted to make Julian jealous instead."

"I know, I know. Relax. That man is your rock, Molly. And you're his soil. You have to *be* with him. We made a grave mistake keeping you two apart for so long. Garrett is worried sick about him. He's been running himself to death. Not eating. Not opening up to anyone. His family feels responsible for this, even his mother is trying to apologize for all her earlier threats, and he won't hear anything from anyone. He's really hurting, Molly. You want him, don't you?"

"You have no idea," she gasped brokenly, nodding so fast she was almost dizzy. The mere idea of being able to see him again was electrifying. Of talking to him. Touching him, even if only with the merest tip of her littlest finger. Oh, God, it hurt so much to love him from afar, reminding her of all the misery of growing up without him.

She had always dreamed of having a family, because hers had been broken before she'd even gotten to know her own parents. She'd just never tried for one of her own because she'd believed Julian would never be a part of it. Now a little kernel of hope sprang in her center, and she opened her eyes.

But she feared to hope too much and end up wretched. "Why?" she asked Kate. "Why is everyone going to help us, after all this time?"

"Because I love you, Molly. And you love him. And *he* loves you. And we all love you both."

Molly coiled her arms around Kate's waist and squeezed her sister as tight as possible, sighing when Kate squeezed her back just as hard. "I miss him so much, Kate."

"I know, Moo. I know you do."

Ten

It was a good day to be at the lake house. Sunny and breezy days on the cusp of summer were hard to come by in Texas. But that was just what the Gage family got when they visited their Canyon Lake home on the last Saturday of the month.

Julian had not planned to set foot here, but Landon had insisted, and he'd grudgingly agreed merely because he would be able to water-ski, swim and do the WaveRunner thing. After a day of that, the only thing that would be aching would be his goddamned muscles rather than his heart.

Now the wind slapped him as he roared across the lake on the WaveRunner, racing Garrett on his right and Landon on his left. He squinted in the direction of the mansion, which stood white and regal by the lake, with a small dock and bright pink bougainvillea hanging from the terrace columns. He could see his mother already seated at the long terrace table, calmly pouring glasses of lemonade for the two figures seated with her—Landon's wife, Beth, and his stepson, David.

Julian swerved and spewed water behind him as he jolted the machine to a stop right beside the dock. He tied up the WaveRunner and jumped out, wet suit soaked, dripping a path up the wood planks as he ambled toward the terrace. When he arrived, he plopped down on a chair and took a glass of lemonade from his mother.

"Landon tells me you're not coming back to the *Daily*," his mother said without preamble. "Are you certain about that?"

Julian nodded, not up to explaining the deal he'd made with Landon and his reasons for it. The point was, he would continue to support the *Daily* with JJG Enterprises' services, personally making sure the *Daily*'s client base thrived. But he was riding solo now.

Eleanor patted her bun absently with one hand, making a puppy-dog plea with her eyes until he groaned. "I've got 1,210 businesses already signed up for the services of JJG Enterprises. *No,* Mother. The *Daily* is my past. I'm a free agent from now on."

She relented quickly, and Julian knew it was due to the guilt that gnawed at her over the way she'd attempted to separate him from Molly over the years, and the pain it had ended up causing him now. In fact, she'd even relented about her threat of cutting off his trust fund because he'd quit the family business, though she was still trying to convince him to come back.

Now his brothers strolled over, wet suits soaked, and plopped down just as a redhead emerged from within the house, carrying a salad bowl.

Julian stiffened at the same time Garrett did.

It must have been the red hair, shining in the sun, flowing behind her in the wind. For a blind second, Julian thought it was Molly. He didn't even know how he felt about that, but his heart kicked in his chest like a wild thing. He was relieved when he realized that it was Kate.

He calmed back down while Garrett went over to take the bowl from her hands and whisper something in her ear.

"Hi, Julian," Kate said, spotting him. "You've been so busy all morning I haven't been able to say hi."

"You just did, so now you can sleep soundly," he said.

Then he realized how grumpy he sounded. Well, hell, he could still tackle some kayaks and hike this afternoon to let out some of his frustration. His every muscle ached, but there was still some juice in them, and he didn't want to have a drop left by the time he was finished. It wasn't enough; he needed to push harder. Push every single muscle to failure.

Servants brought out trays of canapés and wine. While the family chatted, Julian sat in silence, brooding when no second redhead came out of the house. Kate had been invited. So where the hell was Molly?

He wanted to ask, his tongue itching in his mouth. He wanted to ask where she was and how she'd been doing and why in the world she had betrayed him. He'd never gone twenty-three days, four hours, thirty-two minutes and about thirty seconds without talking to her. The time had dragged on so hellishly that it felt like years as far as he was concerned. However he measured it, this was proving to be the crappiest period of his life so far.

Kate kept her attention on him, and he could feel her gaze on his profile as she asked, "You're not going to eat anything?"

Julian stared at the salad bowl. Molly used to get all of his croutons and he'd eat all of her raisins.

He shook his head, not even hungry anymore.

Beth and Landon kept squeezing each other's hands tenderly as they nibbled salad and drank their lemonades, and the grenade inside Julian's stomach seemed to be ready to detonate. His oldest brother had a truly doting wife and a great kid, and he doted on them both in return. The family had been thrilled that Landon had been able to find love again after his first wife and their son had died. They thought he'd closed himself off for good, yet Beth had opened him up like a Christmas present and found gold.

Usually, the sight of them brought Julian immense cheer, but today he found it was…difficult. To see that connection.

Because the only person he'd ever had it with was not with him here.

"So how is dear Molly, Kate?" his mother asked, very politically bringing her up, damn her. "I'm so disappointed she couldn't come."

Lips compressed into a thin line, Julian stared at his empty glass of lemonade, wishing he'd gone for vodka.

"She was disappointed, too," Kate said, "but she had that exhibit in New York and had to fly over for the opening."

Julian refused to think about Molly flying all alone to her solo exhibit. Getting chatted up by someone next to her in first class. By her fans and collectors at the gallery. It was an important time in her career. And Molly had celebrated…alone.

He refused to think about how he should've been there, always had been there.

He restlessly shifted in his seat, trying to console himself with the thought that at least Josh Blackstone, her gallerist, would be there with her. Julian's old acquaintance was as ruthless as a hellhound, but fair with his artists and especially with Molly, whom he'd taken under his wing a long time ago when Julian urged her to submit her works for his consideration.

Blackstone had flipped, called it feisty and fresh, and the rest had been history.

"I've always loved her canvases, my dear. So bright and sunny. Like her. No wonder they do so well in the art market," his mother casually told Kate, and the topic only incensed Julian to a whole new level.

"Remember how she used to save all those wrappers," Garrett added in lingering disbelief. "And twine them around the tree trunks to make some weird..."

"Oh, yeah, the candy tree," Landon said, lifting up his glass. "I think she has one in this exhibition. It's considered to be her 'early work.'"

"Remember that one review?" Beth said, turning to Landon. "You know the one, Lan... Where the reviewer said Molly was the kind of artist who could draw a simple sketch on a paper napkin and sign it and with that, not only pay for her dinner tab, but for the entire restaurant's? Like it was rumored Picasso once did."

The chair legs screeched like angry banshees as Julian pushed back his seat and rose, his face black with rage. With a shove-it-where-it-hurts look, he grabbed his drink to leave.

"Oh, Julian, dear," Eleanor said, "Could you tell one of the servants to bring out the pies?"

He realized his drink was empty and slammed it back down. "Tell them yourself."

Ready to call it quits on family time, he marched toward the dry clothes he'd left on a wood bench by the dock, angrily unzipping and yanking the top part of his wet suit down to his hips. His family kept talking of Molly's artworks, how special they were, and yes, they were incredible pieces, amazing. But it was Molly whom he'd always considered the masterpiece. Living and breathing, coloring his world with passion and liveliness, making his every moment…worthwhile. God, he hated to remember how she used to make him feel.

Stopping in his tracks, he scowled at the wood bench. His clothes were nowhere to be found.

He stormed back to the group. "Where the hell is my stuff?"

Kate covered her cheeks with both hands, eyes wide. "Oh, I'm sorry! I hung everything in the closet at the cottage so it wouldn't get wet or wrinkled."

He rolled his eyes and stomped down the path to the spare cottage a good distance from the main house. Once he got there, he slammed the door shut behind him to keep the AC inside and went to the closet.

That was when he caught a shadow moving out of the corner of his eye.

He did a forty-five-degree turn and saw Molly. She stood by the window, like a virgin fire princess ready for the sacrifice of her life, her hair molten lava running down her rounded shoulders, wearing a sexy little strapless dress and glittery sandals, big earrings, big bangles and a big smile.

His body, traitorous, jumped to life at the sight of her as though *twenty-three* miserable, endless days of continual physical exertion were not enough to keep it numb. Oh, no, not around her. Her mere presence had flicked on his power switch. Now his blood rushed through his veins and his mind sparked to awareness, taking in every detail of her porcelain skin, her pale blue eyes, her shiny hair, her sweet, white, tiny little teeth she'd used to bite him lovingly. He took in every detail now only to torture himself with them later.

His palms itched, his breath hitched, and he said, "You."

He heard shuffling outside the door, and then the sound of a bolt sliding into place.

Plunk.

And he realized too late, that his family had just locked him in with her.

"Me," Molly agreed calmly.

And suddenly it didn't matter that Julian obviously didn't want to be here, that he didn't want to see her. It didn't matter that his eyes flashed reproachfully at her, that his stance was wide and defensive, that his lips were hard and pressed together in anger. The sight of him after all these painful days made her lungs throb and her head spin with the sheer joy of being able to look at him.

And he looked extremely good.

His torso was damp with lake water and tanned by the sun. His chest looked wider, his athletic form so incredibly sexy in the way the wet suit hung halfway down his body, emphasizing his narrow hips and waist. The shiny black fabric clung seductively to his thighs and to the promi-nent part of him that had once joined him with her. His hair was damp and slicked back from his face, revealing every inch of his formidable features. The features of a playboy, a Greek god, the man she loved—and the man who wanted nothing to do with her.

Molly trembled with nervousness, desire, regret.

She noticed his hair, still streaked enticingly by the sun, was growing a bit longer, to his nape, and she could smell the woods on him, the oaks and the cedars on the property.

"I thought you had a show," he said, his tone indicating that he didn't really care about her answer.

She still wanted to tell him—because he used to be the only one who truly listened—that it had gone well, that the reviews were excellent and everyone thought she was the luckiest person on earth to have succeeded so young. They thought she had it all.

But she didn't.

She didn't have what she wanted most. Had always wanted.

"I got back from the opening yesterday," she said slowly, her hands restless at her sides, fiddling with the skirt of her dress. "Everyone seemed to like my paintings, except for my two most depressing ones." *The ones that suck because of you.*

"You have no depressing works," he said, pointing at her.

He pursed his lips as he once again scanned his surroundings. Then he shook his head in disgust, marched back to the closet, yanked open the doors and began to pull out his clothes briskly from the hangers.

She felt an unwelcome rush of desire when he began to change right before her eyes. He pulled off his wet suit with a snap, and when he peeled it from his thighs and kicked it off, she saw his nude backside. Glorious muscles rippled and clenched as he put on his Boss underwear and khaki pants. He slipped on a polo shirt and buttoned the two top buttons, then crossed the room toward the cottage door and tried to force the knob. He cursed under his breath when it didn't open and angrily swung around to her.

"So you're into kidnapping now, Molls? Is that your new kick?"

"Yes, as a matter of fact, I'm into spanking, kidnapping and robbing unsuspecting clients of their money while I fail to complete their murals."

Jaw clamped, he stormed to one of the windows and attempted to open it so forcibly the glass rattled in its frame. He acted as if he was in prison and eager to be set free, which just made Molly sigh in despair.

"Look, this wasn't my idea, but I think the plan is brilliant," she said.

"Except for one flaw," he said wickedly, unlocking a second window with a surprising click. He cocked a devil-may-care brow at her and grinned as he pushed upward, only to realize there was another lock on the outside and the glass stayed right in place, no matter how hard he tried to get it open. *"Damn."*

"You don't want to talk to me, Julian, that's fine," Molly said softly. "But I need to talk to you. So now you're going to have to hear me out. Even if you *break* one of those windows, Jules, what are you planning to do? Let in some fresh air?"

He scowled as she pointed at the forged-iron bars on the outside.

"Your mother had that design made specially to keep the drunk teenagers from getting in like they've been doing at other lake houses, and if they can't come in through those bars, I doubt even *you* can go out through them."

The glare he shot her could've been Lucifer's. "I can't believe this idiocy. First they don't want me near you, now they lock me up with you?"

Shaking his head, he paced like a caged lion.

His tumultuous energy spun through the room like a whirlwind, making her want to go over there, wrap her arms around him and calm him down like she had many times before when he was irritated about other things.

But now he saw her as untrustworthy, and he wouldn't want to open up. Now his irritation was caused by the fact that he was locked in the same room as Molly.

"Your family has realized we're miserable and they're trying to make amends. Well, *I* have been miserable," she added, watching him pace. "Jules, will you please look at me so I can talk to you? Or do I need to call you JJ to make you react?"

He stopped in his tracks, his hands curling at his sides, fingers clenching. Although his face was a mask of cold indifference, his eyes blazed with intensity. "Don't even think about provoking me."

"Or you'll what? Kiss me?"

His glare was as bleak as a cemetery. "I'll spank the hell out of you, how about that? I'm *through* with kissing you, Molls."

The decisiveness in his words summoned a fresh wave of outrage from her. "Really? And who says I even *want* you to?"

"A closed door with a lock on it, that's who!" His teeth were clenched so tight, she could see a muscle twitch in the back of his jaw.

She glowered at him, but feared in the innermost part of her, where a candle of hope flickered its last lights, that this battle was already lost. Apparently, not only was her presence not wanted, her kiss was worth nothing to him, either. But she, on the other hand, remembered perfectly all the things she had done as a result of *his* masquerade kiss. "So are you going to listen to me, *JJ?* God, I'm trying to fix things here!" she cried.

He looked up at the ceiling and pinched his eyes shut as though supremely tested. She thought she heard him counting under his breath, stopping at thirty-eight, his hands still clenching and unclenching.

Gradually, he turned around to plant his hands on the wall, then stared out the window with his forehead almost touching the glass pane. His voice was a coarsened whisper. "I'm damned well listening. So talk."

Molly dragged in a breath as she watched his hands splay wider on the wall. She longed to feel those fingers again, feel him touch her, caress her, hold her. "Garrett wanted to talk to me that day I went to his office. He wanted to discuss our relationship."

His hands fisted against the window frame. "Whose?" he asked, his knuckles white. "His and yours?"

"Yours and mine, Jules." She flung her hands up in exasperation. "Obviously! So I told him—"

He spun around like a cyclone. "You told him that I was leaving the *Daily,* and my family could have ruined everything I've planned for years. What *else* did you tell him? You were fishing for his approval by ratting me out, weren't you?"

The hurt that exploded in Molly's chest was so massive that she almost staggered. "Do you really believe that? *Do you?*" Her voice sounded panicked, but she didn't care.

The look he shot back at her was so raw and stark it all but extinguished her candle of hope.

Her voice broke, and she opened her hands out in silent plea. "Look, I'm sorry, Jules. It wasn't on purpose. I was angry about the way they tried to warn me off you and wasn't even thinking clearly. Please, please help me out here. I'm so in love with you I just can't bear this anymore."

"That information wasn't yours to share and *especially* not with them, Moo!" He shook his head and plunged a hand into his damp hair. "Look, I just can't talk to you now. I can't. I'm too goddamned pissed that you would…" A halting hand shot up in the air when she started forward, and she abruptly stopped, her heart in her throat.

He sighed and backed away from her, and every step he took felt like a mile she would never be able to recover. He took a seat on the window bench, and Molly eased back and ended up alone on a floral couch, silent and hurt.

He didn't say he loves me back was all she could think. *God, please, doesn't he care for me just a little bit anymore?*

She thought of how easily he had jumped between lovers and beds his entire life and she wondered if there had been women warming his bed all this time, comforting him while she'd been pining for him alone, producing the worst artworks of her life because of him.

Seduce him, a little voice whispered. *Make him forgive you.*

But the thought made her feel cheap and as fake as he thought her to be. How could she go through with a seduction? First of all, he wasn't even giving any indication that he still *wanted* her. And it had never been just about sex between them. It had been about friendship and fun and sharing and trust....

Trust.

Once long ago, Molly had been careless and had broken Eleanor Gage's prized crystal figurine, one up on display over the chimney mantel. No matter how Julian tried to help her fix it, the thing could never be properly glued back together without looking pitifully disfigured. Now the thought that she could have shattered Julian's trust just like that dolphin figurine, a figurine they'd ended up *throwing away,* terrified her.

Despair made her sink deeper into her own personal bubble. She'd always felt strong in her life, plunging into adventures without thinking too much about their consequences. But now the source of her strength was gone, and she felt totally lost without him.

The sun began to set outside, the lights of dusk bathing the room in a golden glow. She wondered if some woman had been stroking Julian's Beckham-blond hair a day before. If a woman with model legs and bigger breasts had been feeling his beautiful hands on her skin and sighing under his searing kisses. His beautiful kisses.

"Have you been sleeping around again?" she blurted

out, unable to stand the torment of wondering about it any longer. The jealousy was ripping her insides into shreds.

"I don't feel like sex ever since you and I—" He glared, as though furious he'd revealed as much. Eyebrows pulled downward, he then growled, *"No."*

The relief she felt made her sag back against the couch.

"Have *you?*" he shot back.

"Of course not!" she cried.

His narrowed gaze held hers with magnetic force, and they both fell so quiet that Molly could've heard a pin drop across the room. Unable to bear the strength of his stare, she broke eye contact and surveyed her sandaled feet, her stomach roiling. God, how she missed his oak leaf–green eyes.

"So do they plan to leave us here all night?" Sounding just as thrilled as he had minutes ago—which was not thrilled *at all*—Julian looked around the cozy cottage as though he still hoped to find an escape route.

It made Molly feel about as wanted as an abandoned rug. She nodded dejectedly. "I think they left some food in the kitchenette and water and…champagne."

How foolish to even mention that last item.

As if they would both have something to celebrate. *Uh-huh. Right.*

She had totally underestimated the size of Julian's pride, and the size of her own, and now she just wanted to stop begging and curl up on a pillow and never wake up until the Earth spun the way it was supposed to. The way it used to.

Her eyes blurred as she glanced up at him, but he was looking out the window, still unapproachable, and though she trembled with the urge to feel his arms around her, she curled up on the sofa and grabbed a pillow embroidered with *Home Is Where the Heart Is*. Shutting her eyes tiredly, she cuddled on one corner and strove to pretend Julian wasn't here with her. It was easy. Because she'd never before felt so broken, so somber and so lonely when she was with him.

But then his voice flicked through her, soft and husky enough that she could almost pretend it was a caress.

"Do you remember when you flunked your second driving test, Molly?"

She nodded, throat tightening. He had to bring that up.

"Do you remember taking out Landon's car for a little practice drive and crashing the hell out of it?"

She nodded faster, her throat tightening even more.

"You pulled me out of a damn Spurs game in the final period. And I fixed things. Fixed them so that you'd never be caught, gladly taking the super-fun lecture from my brother and mother for you. I never ratted you out. Never."

Throat burning thick now, she kept her eyes closed and prayed he didn't notice the dampness in her lashes, the tears stealing from between her eyelids to slide down her cheeks and to the pillow. "I'm sorry," she gritted out helplessly, opening her eyes to see the blurry vision of him. "You've always been my hero. I'm *sorry* I turned out to be the villain in *your* plot!"

He laughed, a sarcastic sound that said he didn't even care, and then he said no more and leaned a shoulder on the window and stared outside, probably wishing he was anywhere but here. With her.

"If we hadn't slept together," she asked his profile, "would you still be my best friend and talk to me?"

He rubbed one of his arms absently over his chest as he continued staring out the window. "Ask Garrett to be your bud," he said quietly.

Her eyebrows furrowed, and the anger and injustice that had been building up in her for days overtook her in an explosion. She jumped to her feet, shaking in fury. "You know what, Jules? Go to hell! If you want to hang on to the one thing I've done wrong to you in my life, that's your call. But you know I've been there for you every single second of your life like your own private cheerleader. If you had a fan club you know damned well I'd be the *president*. I happen to think that there's no one in the world as perfectly wonderful and special and incredible as you. But if you think that I would willingly hurt you in any way, for *anyone* else, even your brothers, then you're an idiot. And you don't deserve me *or* my friendship, much less my *love!*"

She was just too hurt and too tired to beg anymore. She'd thought what Julian and she had would survive anything. That they were invincible and powerful.

And now here they were, strangers and almost enemies, as if they hadn't once meant everything to each other.

He didn't reply to her words, but kept staring stiffly out the window, his profile taut.

Molly sighed and dropped back to the sofa, tired from her trip, from twenty-three days without sleep, weeks of wishing to find love and losing everything precious in her life in the process. Tired and frustrated, she tossed and turned on the couch, and she did that until finally sleep took over.

During the night her eyes fluttered open to see him still sitting by the window. Every time she looked, she found those green eyes watching her in the darkness.

The last time she woke up shivering and confused, and when she saw him still sitting there, alone and watching her with eyes that were almost as shadowed as the room, she curled herself into a ball and groggily said, "You should get some sleep, Jules. You can keep on hating me tomorrow."

He started coming over with something in his hands. "People with insomnia don't sleep, Molls," he murmured, and covered her with a blanket.

And that was as close as he got to her.

Eleven

It was past 7:00 a.m. when Julian heard someone fiddling with the outside bolt, and he stalked across the room like a man chasing a diabolical fiend. He'd slept exactly zero hours, had been torn between taking Molly in his arms and breaking a freaking window with his fist, but he would be damned if he gave his family the satisfaction of doing either.

No. He was through doing whatever they wanted him to do.

They thought he and Molly would have something to celebrate? The only thing Julian was going to celebrate today was ramming his fist into his brothers' jaws.

And that was exactly what he did as soon as the bolt was removed and he pushed the cottage door open to find Garrett outside, turning to leave.

"Good morning," Julian said to make his brother turn back around. He did.

And the force Julian put into his punch was so heavy it floored him instantly. Garrett smacked the ground with a loud thump.

Inside the cottage, Molly jumped to her feet with a start, her eyes wide and startled as she came over and saw the middle Gage brother sprawled at Julian's feet. She whipped her face up to him and fiercely scowled. "Oh, you were just itching to do that, weren't you? You've been talking about your guns for months!"

Frowning, Julian stretched out his fingers in confusion, because damn, that had hurt. Apparently, Garrett was too hardheaded to punch without getting a bit of a jolt in his knuckles, too.

"Yeah," Julian admitted to her. Then he glowered down at his brother and nudged him with his foot. "That felt real good, you son of a bitch!"

Coming up to a sitting position, Garrett wiped the blood off his mouth with the sleeve of his polo shirt and spat out the rest. "We have the same mother, you *moron*."

"I'm going home," he heard Molly mutter under her breath as she stormed toward the terrace, where Julian watched her grab some keys from Kate's purse. A minute later the catering van was pulling out of the driveway.

He wanted to chase her, yell and fight with her, the adrenaline was so off the charts in his body. But his instinct to spare her his rage was still too strong, and he was more bloodthirsty to make his brother his outlet for his rage.

Garrett was pushing to his feet, but Julian didn't let him. He shoved him back down by bracing one knee on his shoulder. "Stop meddling in our lives! We're not your responsibility, or Mother's or anyone else's. And if we wanted to be together, we sure as hell have never needed your idiotic help!"

Garrett pushed him aside and shuffled to his feet, rubbing his sore jaw. "She loves you, Jules. You're being an ass."

"Make that a headline in the paper tomorrow, brother. See if I buy a copy." Julian stalked away and flipped Garrett his two middle fingers without even glancing backward.

"Argh, you hardheaded bastard." Garrett pounced, scowling as he blocked his path. "You're going to make me fight you, aren't you?" Gritting his teeth in obvious frustration, his older brother began rolling up his sleeves.

"Get out of my way," Julian warned.

"Molly didn't betray you, you imbecile! She was furious because we were warning her away from you. She didn't *know* we've been riding you about her for years and she was trying to defend you. Why can you not *see* that?"

Julian wasn't listening. He was still restless, reckless, seething.

All night. All night, watching inches and inches of goose-bump-covered, creamy white skin, lustrous red hair and parted pink lips. All night, torturing himself with wanting her so damned much. He'd had a hard-on for hours. Hours.

"You know that girl loves you more than anyone or anything in this world. Don't you? *Don't you, Julian?*" Garrett demanded.

He glared at his brother. Goddammit, he wished he was sure of her. That she did not want anyone else. That she would never put any other man before him, ever again, before *Julian*.

"And you love her so bad you were ready to dump your whole family just to be with her," Garrett insisted.

Julian was suddenly incensed. "Because she's mine. Mine. Always has been. Always will be. She gave me her damned lollipop, and I took it, and right then and there—she was mine, Garrett. *Mine.*"

"Well, then. Why are you here arguing with me while she's on her way home?"

Julian dropped his face with a grimace of pain, remembering her words as he rubbed his throbbing temples. *Please, please help me out here. I'm so in love with you I can't bear this anymore.*

If only he could be absolutely sure that she truly loved him. *Him.*

Not…his brother.

"Well? Are you going to let her get away now that you have her?" Garrett pressed as he signaled at the empty driveway. "Do you think a good girl like Molly would be with you if she wasn't all for you, man?"

Julian stared off to where she'd disappeared. "She was never with me."

"Come again?"

"Molly. It was a lie. Our relationship. She was never really with me. She wanted…you."

Just saying that to Garrett made him feel sick to his empty stomach. He didn't even know how he could have gone along with her foolish plan in the first place.

"Sooooo…*that's* what this is about." Garrett threw his head back and released one of his few real laughs, the sound booming across the landscape. "Molly doesn't want me, Jules. Hell, I sure as hell would know when a woman does." His gaze strayed over to Kate. She was speaking to their mother by the docks, and Garrett watched her for a long, long moment, his eyes on fire with emotion.

He jerked back when he realized he was being watched and growled, "Molly's loved you her whole life, jerk. She wanted to marry you when she was younger. She thought when it was time for her prom, she would be taking *you.*

Kate had to tell her once and for all that she should see you as a brother and start thinking of another boy to invite to prom. She cried for days because she'd never be able to marry you. She even packed her bags and that feisty little girl actually tried to *leave*—said she didn't want to grow up with us and have you as a brother. Our mother forced her to stay, but can you please understand how Mother would remain concerned about this development?"

It took a moment for him to absorb this. He imagined Molly in all her stages. Never once had any man featured in any of them—except for Julian. While he'd known he could never have her and had sought to fill in the void with a thousand different women, she had done the opposite and had wanted no man.

Until one kiss from Julian had awakened her.

God, if he had known that all this time... All. This. Time. She'd wanted to go to *prom* with him? Had wanted to *marry* him?

She'd been his friend, and he'd been hers, and neither had realized that they had truly ever only loved and wanted each other.

His heart soared at the realization, and for the first time in days, he felt as if he could take a normal breath again. But he still glared at his brother for having made his life a living hell where Molly was concerned. "Clearly what you all failed to see is that I *loved* her. I always have, you morons."

Brow rising in interest, Garrett stopped pretending to roll up his sleeves and now began to roll them down. "Oh, well, then. So what are you doing here?"

Julian stared out at the placid lake, and then once again noticed how Garrett kept glancing at Kate on the docks. "You plan to give me advice, old man," Julian dared, pointing at her. "And yet I don't see you following your own. I know you want her, Garrett, I'm not blind. Why don't you freaking do something?"

Garrett stiffened, his face harsh and pained. "The difference between you and me is that you've always known you deserve Molly. And I'll never deserve Kate."

Every muscle tense with longing, Julian thought of Molly as she'd been last night, how vulnerable she'd looked as she slept, how she'd shivered and how he'd watched her, covered her with a blanket while he'd wanted to cover her with his body instead. All night. All night he'd spent memorizing her face, wanting to pretend this little beauty had not hurt him like she had.

If you had a fan club you know damned well I'd be the president!

How adorable she'd looked, ranting at him. And he'd been an ass. Unreasonable and closed off to her, not even listening, letting his anger and that damned feeling of jealousy overcome him.

His heart began to race at the thought of losing her, really losing her, for life. No. Never. Because Molly was smarter than he was, and she would not cling to the one thing he'd done wrong in his life. She was better than that.

And he was getting her back. He had to, and this time it would be for life. His heart swelled as he thought of her. His little Moo, his Mo-Po, his Mopey, his Molls, his Picasso, his *Molly*. The one he'd always wanted, with all her paint-streaked skin, frilly skirt and sassy attitude that got her into trouble.

No, Molly had not betrayed him to Garrett intentionally, or out of preference for the other man. She'd been too innocent for her own damn good, which was why she'd always needed Julian in the first place. He'd be damned if his pride and anger and jealousy would keep her away from him now.

"You're right," he said, resolute. "I do deserve Molly, or at least I did."

He started across the gravel path, suddenly wanting to get his favorite pair of Nikes and run like the wind to her home. But then, his Aston Martin was probably faster.

"I'll just go and put some ice on this," Garrett called after him sarcastically, rubbing his jaw.

"I have a better idea. Why don't you let Kate do it," Julian yelled in return, and began sprinting to his car, his heart galloping. He would tear her clothes off when he saw her. He would nibble, lick and kiss her until she couldn't stand it and begged for him to stop. And then he'd stop, only to do it all over again.

His heart pounded as he drove, his mind homing in on one thing, just one thing.

He could barely feel the pain in his muscles now, the synapses in his brain all firing on one word, one thought, one girl.

Outside her place, he grabbed the key they hid in the planter, opened the front door and slammed it shut. He could hear his own footsteps echo as he charged down the hallway to her room.

Her door was open a crack, and he stopped. All of a sudden his system was ready to go haywire, and he wanted to do everything at once.

When he entered her room, he saw her lying facedown on her bed, as if she'd been crying or just tired or—God, he hoped she hadn't been crying.

As he quietly backed out of the room, she sat upright with a start.

Then she saw him and leaped to her feet, her gaze throwing daggers at him. Gone were her earrings, her bangles and her smile. Despite her obvious anger, he was about to detonate with hunger and love for this passionate little redhead. He reversed course and advanced on her with slow purpose, like that night at the masquerade, with the single-minded determination of a man truly possessed. By love, by desire, by a woman. By *his* woman.

She continued to look fiercely at him. "Go back to fight with your brother, Julian," she snapped.

Julian paused in the middle of the hall and spread out his arms in a gesture of pure innocence. "I'd much rather fight with you, Moo."

"Well, I *wouldn't.* I don't plan to fight with you anymore."

He smiled the smile he knew to be irresistible to her, his hands up in the air as if she'd trained a loaded gun on him. "All right, then. Let's make up. What do you say?"

She opened her mouth to answer, then shut it.

At the first sign of her hesitation, Julian dropped his arms and started forward. "I'm so sorry, baby."

She shook her head. "You don't say you're sorry, Julian John. You bring flowers and say, 'Here are your flowers and look outside, there's another truckful for you.'"

"Damn, you're greedy, Moo. I'll get you a whole flower shop as soon as I get my hands off you."

Lines of confusion settled across her features, and suddenly her lips quirked at the ends. "You can't get them off me if you don't have them *on* me, Jules."

"Count to three." He could literally *see* her lovely baby blues start to glow for him once more.

"One," she suddenly whispered.

His heart turned over in his chest, and he almost fell to his knees from his gratitude to her. Struggling to find words, his voice came out rough and uneven. "I'm sorry I was so damned jealous and unreasonable, but please understand there's not a woman in the world who drives me as crazy as you do. I couldn't stand the thought of you siding with them, of you putting my brother before me in any way. The thought of you responding to him like you respond to me—"

"Jules, no one has ever come before you. It wasn't *him* I responded to that first night you kissed me, it was *you*. I realized right away that I was kissing my soul mate."

He charged toward her. "I want to spend the rest of my life with you, Molly, and I want to know that I will always be your first and foremost, because you're sure as hell mine."

She lunged forward. "Two, three!"

He laughed in pure male thrill when he opened his arms at the same time Molly leaped and curled herself around him. *"I love you,"* she murmured, open-lipped against him.

He slanted his head and fitted his mouth to hers, a sound of desperation and hunger rumbling up from his throat. Molly met this sound with her own breathless gasp, her fingers delving into his hair until he could feel the delicious bite of her nails on his scalp.

Oh, baby, yeah.

He could feel her kiss in his every living cell, she kissed him so thoroughly, so completely. He hungrily squeezed her buttocks as he suckled her tongue and almost drowned in the taste of mint and apples and Mopey.

"I missed you so bad I haven't even been myself," he growled. Ducking his head to her breasts, he pulled down her strapless dress to find them bare and waiting for him. He suctioned a nipple between his teeth and closed his eyes as bliss pummeled him from the inside.

"Jules, I could've killed you for being such a hard-headed, moronic—"

"Shh." His head came up and he silenced her with a fingertip. "Be nice to me or I won't do this, hmm." He stuck his finger into her mouth and she suckled it greedily while he watched, his eyes feeling heavy.

She mewed in protest when he retrieved his finger, so then he used his lips to part hers wider and thrust his hot, wet tongue inside her. "Please tell me I didn't make you cry, baby," he desperately whispered as he broke their kiss for a moment to slant his head and get a better angle.

She nodded, speaking into his mouth as she gloried in the taste of him. "Like eleven times."

"Now I'll have to make it up to my girl with an hour of this for every time I made her cry." He cupped her breasts lovingly and kissed each one with care.

Molly panted, quivering with arousal as his skillful hands gripped the fabric of her dress at her hips and pulled it over her head, leaving her in her lacy black panties.

"It was really more like thirty-five times. I just didn't want to sound desperate," she confessed, her voice full of yearning as she fondled his dampened lips with her fingertips.

"Poor baby." He drew back to take a good look at her, his eyelids heavy as he caressed her lovely curves with his fingers. "Let me get my math straight…how many times?"

"A hundred times," she concluded, her breasts jerking up and down with her laboring breaths as she tightened her legs around his hips.

"A hundred times that I made my baby cry… I have a lot of making up to do."

Molly shuddered at the words, at the way he muttered them against her swollen breast, the way he laved her nipples and then breathed on them until she thought she would burst.

She'd been waiting for him, praying and plotting and planning to get him back. The one and only man for her.

A little hardheaded, true. But to her, Julian John Gage was still the bomb. The *bomb*.

Now he was here, in her arms, and she never wanted him to leave.

She held her breath as she frantically pulled his shirt over his head, and when he sent it flying across the room, his magnificent muscles bulged.

"I was about to call Garrett and ask him to pretend to love me." She rubbed his hard, square shoulders and delighted over the satin feel of his skin. "Just to see if you came back around."

"Oh, yeah?"

His smile was all cocky as he set her on her feet, then he hooked a finger in her panties and pulled them down, off one leg, then the other. "The difference is," he said as he undid his belt buckle and sent it clattering to the floor, "that he would be pretending. While I never was."

Once he was naked, he kicked the door shut and boosted her up against the wall, guiding her legs around his hips. Molly locked her ankles at the small of his back, clenching him tight between her arms and thighs and never planning to let go. His eyes glowed so bright and tender on her face, the light warmed her to the very depths of her being.

"Make love with me?" he murmured.

She jerked her head breathlessly as he held her hips between his big hands, and then, as sunlight streamed in through her bedroom window and their eyes locked, he thrust inside of her. She cried out with the joy of being physically his again. She'd been so ready to settle for friendship, if that was all she'd get. But in the deepest, most secret parts of her, she had ached for so much more.

"Jules, love me. Say you love me."

"I love you like crazy." He framed her face and looked

into her eyes. "Never doubt it. I love you, I worship you, I adore you, Molly. You and you alone."

His passionate words drove her to the precipice. They came together with tempestuous force, and once their endless shudders subsided, Molly gasped and turned her face into his neck, struggling to catch her breath. She'd felt his warmth spill into her, had felt the powerful contractions that seized his body, and now her heart soared in the sheer joy of being entwined with Julian again.

Panting and sweaty, she lifted her head just as he was ducking to kiss her. Their lips met in a languorous, loving, lazy kiss that left her weak and buzzing. "Every time you kiss me," she said softly, stroking his face as he carried her to the bed, "it feels like the first time." A dreamy sigh escaped her as she remembered that masquerade. "I should've *known* I was being kissed by a playboy."

"Get used to it, Mopey." He set her down on the mattress with a kiss on her forehead, then stretched out beside her and rumpled her hair. "Because I promise you'll never see a playboy more into his wife than I."

Her heart stuttered at the word *wife,* then it just completely stopped beating.

"What do you mean?"

At the sight of her wide eyes, his wolfish smile appeared, and he took her left hand within his. She watched in disbelief as he slid the matte platinum ring, large and masculine, onto her ring finger.

The ring from the masquerade.

"I'll get you a real one tomorrow. One with a white diamond—a big one. This is just so you know my intentions are pure."

"Oh, I have no doubt your intentions are squeaky clean," she laughed as she pointedly glanced down at their nakedness, and then she fell somber as the magnitude of what was happening struck her. Settling her hands on his shoulders, she gazed at the ring, then into those oak leaf-green eyes. She could see his pulse fluttering rapidly at the base of his throat, could see the love and need in his eyes.

"You were meant to be my wife, Molly," he rasped, brushing her hair back, his hands, his tenderness undoing her. "Will you marry me?"

She held his caressing green gaze and nodded, her eyes mirroring the loving way that Julian looked down at her now. Stroking his strong jaw affectionately, she simply said, "As you wish."

* * * * *

Look for Kate's story, coming soon!
Only from Red Garnier and Harlequin Desire!

REQUEST YOUR FREE BOOKS!
2 FREE NOVELS PLUS 2 FREE GIFTS!

ALWAYS POWERFUL, PASSIONATE AND PROVOCATIVE

YES! Please send me 2 FREE Harlequin Desire® novels and my 2 FREE gifts (gifts are worth about $10). After receiving them, if I don't wish to receive any more books, I can return the shipping statement marked "cancel." If I don't cancel, I will receive 6 brand-new novels every month and be billed just $4.55 per book in the U.S. or $4.99 per book in Canada. That's a savings of at least 13% off the cover price! It's quite a bargain! Shipping and handling is just 50¢ per book in the U.S. and 75¢ per book in Canada.* I understand that accepting the 2 free books and gifts places me under no obligation to buy anything. I can always return a shipment and cancel at any time. Even if I never buy another book, the two free books and gifts are mine to keep forever.

225/326 HDN F4ZC

Name	(PLEASE PRINT)

Address	Apt. #

City	State/Prov.	Zip/Postal Code

Signature (if under 18, a parent or guardian must sign)

Mail to the **Harlequin® Reader Service:**
IN U.S.A.: P.O. Box 1867, Buffalo, NY 14240-1867
IN CANADA: P.O. Box 609, Fort Erie, Ontario L2A 5X3

Want to try two free books from another line?
Call 1-800-873-8635 or visit www.ReaderService.com.

* Terms and prices subject to change without notice. Prices do not include applicable taxes. Sales tax applicable in N.Y. Canadian residents will be charged applicable taxes. Offer not valid in Quebec. This offer is limited to one order per household. Not valid for current subscribers to Harlequin Desire books. All orders subject to credit approval. Credit or debit balances in a customer's account(s) may be offset by any other outstanding balance owed by or to the customer. Please allow 4 to 6 weeks for delivery. Offer available while quantities last.

Your Privacy—The Harlequin® Reader Service is committed to protecting your privacy. Our Privacy Policy is available online at www.ReaderService.com or upon request from the Harlequin Reader Service.

We make a portion of our mailing list available to reputable third parties that offer products we believe may interest you. If you prefer that we not exchange your name with third parties, or if you wish to clarify or modify your communication preferences, please visit us at www.ReaderService.com/consumerschoice or write to us at Harlequin Reader Service Preference Service, P.O. Box 9062, Buffalo, NY 14269. Include your complete name and address.

SPECIAL EXCERPT FROM

 HARLEQUIN®

Desire

A sneak peek at

STERN, *a Westmoreland novel*

by New York Times *and* USA TODAY *bestselling author*

Brenda Jackson

Available September 2013.
Only from Harlequin® Desire!

As far as Stern was concerned, his best friend had lost her ever-loving mind. But he didn't say that. Instead, he asked, "What's his name?"

"You don't need to know that. Do you tell me the name of every woman you want?"

"This is different."

"Really? In what way?"

He wasn't sure, but he just knew that it was. "For you to even ask me, that means you're not ready for the kind of relationship you're going after."

JoJo threw her head back and laughed. "Stern, I'll be thirty next year. I'm beginning to think that most of the men in town wonder if I'm really a girl."

He studied her. There had never been any doubt in his mind that she was a girl. She had long lashes and eyes so dark they were the color of midnight. She had gorgeous legs, long and endless. But he knew he was one of the few men who'd ever seen them.

"You hide what a nice body you have," he finally said. He suddenly sat up straight in the rocker. "I have an idea.

What you need is a makeover."

"A makeover?"

"Yes, and then you need to go where your guy hangs out. In a dress that shows your legs, in a style that shows off your hair." He reached over and took the cap off her head. Lustrous dark brown hair tumbled to her shoulders. He smiled. "See, I like it already."

And he did. He was tempted to run his hands through it to feel the silky texture.

He leaned back and took another sip of his beer, wondering where such a tempting thought had come from. This was JoJo, for heaven's sake. His best friend. He should not be thinking about how silky her hair was.

He should not be bothered by the thought of men checking out JoJo, of men calling her for a date.

Suddenly, he was thinking that maybe a makeover wasn't such a great idea after all.

Will Stern help JoJo win her dream man?

STERN

by New York Times *and* USA TODAY
bestselling author Brenda Jackson

*Available September 2013
Only from Harlequin® Desire!*

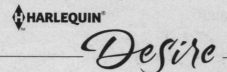

HARLEQUIN®
Desire

ALWAYS POWERFUL, PASSIONATE AND PROVOCATIVE.

CONVENIENTLY
HIS PRINCESS

Olivia Gates

**Part of the Married by Royal Decree series:
When the king commands, they say "I do!"**

Aram's convenient bride turns out to be most
inconvenient when he falls in love with her! But will
Kanza believe in their love when the truth comes out?

Find out next month in
CONVENIENTLY HIS PRINCESS by Olivia Gates,
only from Harlequin® Desire.

Available wherever books and ebooks are sold.

HD73268